A Magical Christmas Wedding

Jen Lowry

Monarch Educational Services, L.L.C.
Clayton, NC

A Magical Christmas Wedding
by Jen Lowry

Cover Designer: The Magic Quill Graphics by Jessica Ozment

https://jenlowrywrites.com/   @jenlowrywrites
A Magical Christmas Wedding/Jen Lowry. – First Edition 2019
Library of Congress Control Number: 2019913999
Summary: Mackenzie and Jordan are days away from their Christmas
wedding. Mac finds herself with more than cold feet. She travels back to
1955. Will she make it back in time to marry the man of her dreams or will
she never find a way back home?

ISBN for paperback version: ISBN: 978-1-7331381-7-8
{1. Christian Fiction 2. Supernatural Fiction 3. Fantasy 4. Clean Romance
5. Christianity 6. Faith 7. Time Travel 8. Christmas 9. Wedding 10.
Holiday 11. Family Drama 12. Romance 13. Diverse

Typography by Monarch Educational Services, L.L.C.

7 6 5 4 3 2 1

Monarch Educational Services, L.L.C.
Clayton NC

A Magical Christmas Wedding

Jen Lowry

Monarch Educational Services, L.L.C.
Clayton NC

Books by Jen Lowry

Children's Books
Dear God, Please Take Care of Rambo
Myrtle's Garden

MG Fiction
My Boyfriend's Back Angels in Love Series
Lyric Harper & the Harmonic Bridge
The Raptor Revolution Save Christmas Mountain

YA Fiction
The Hartwell Chronicles Teenage Exorcist Series
Bridges The Lightbearers Series
Sweet Potato Jones (Swoon Romance, 2020)

Poetry
The Clay in the Potter's Hands: Southern Poetry

Dr. Jennifer Ikner Lowry
Challenge Devotional Series
Happy Renewal Year
Everyday Mom Challenge
30 Day Teacher Challenge
Fingerprint Curriculum

To Eli, for dreaming with me
To Solomon and Samuel, my loves forever

The Road Not Taken
By Robert Frost

Two roads diverged in a yellow wood,
And sorry I could not travel both
And be one traveler, long I stood
And looked down one as far as I could
To where it bent in the undergrowth;

Then took the other, as just as fair,
And having perhaps the better claim,
Because it was grassy and wanted wear;
Though as for that the passing there
Had worn them really about the same,

And both that morning equally lay
In leaves no step had trodden black.
Oh, I kept the first for another day!
Yet knowing how way leads on to way,
I doubted if I should ever come back.

I shall be telling this with a sigh
Somewhere ages and ages hence:
Two roads diverged in a wood, and I—
I took the one less travelled by,
And that has made all the difference.

Dear Reader

I know the foreword usually goes at the beginning of a book, and it's written by someone other than the author. So, I'm not calling this a foreword and simply wanted to write you a letter. I wanted to share with you what's on my heart about *A Magical Christmas Wedding* before you meet Mac and Jordan and all the characters in this book I love. I wanted to tell you about who I wrote this book for, so you'd understand.

This book is dedicated to my mother, Betty Lou. I think she would've loved this book because it has that holiday television feel she absolutely adored and looked forward to each year. When the Christmas romance specials started airing on television, we'd pile in her little tv room and watch movies for hours. If she saw a new commercial for an upcoming night of holiday romance, she'd call me, and we'd schedule a viewing together! Even if we'd seen them the year before, we'd catch them again. Let's get real here. We'd have those babies on repeat.

When I saw that *Hallmark* had open submissions to accept novels in September, I set right away to form the challenge to write a book for my Mesa (her nickname – table in Spanish). The more my life called, and I was learning how to balance my back to school schedule (teaching full time and homeschooling at night), I knew I wouldn't meet the deadline. That's when the story actually developed into what it was supposed to be all along - a Christian fiction holiday story!

You'll get to meet Mac and Jordan today. I'm excited about that because you'll get to live in a world for a few hours that the Holy Spirit gave me in honor of my mother. You're sharing this with me, and I'm so humbled you've chosen this to read out of the tons of other holiday romances.

My mother passed away with lung disease (COPD) from years of smoking. Since her passing, I've not been able to watch a holiday movie we shared together. I pretty much turned from all things romance and moved over into the horror/paranormal genre I love. Last year, during the Christmas season, I cried all the way through watching *You've Got Mail.* That was once my daily December dose of love, my happy place movie. I made it through the movie and told my husband, Eli, during the year of 2019 I might be able to watch a *Hallmark* movie again. I felt it could be part of my healing.

In 2019, I watched *The Shop Around the Corner* with Eli. He held my hand through it. It's the original, black and white, Jimmy Stewart movie that inspired *You've Got Mail.* My Daddy ordered me the movie on VHS because I loved it so much, and he'd watch it with me. I made it through that movie in 2019. I knew there was hope for me yet.

Now we are approaching the holiday season, and I can smile knowing I contributed to the line of Christmas romance books, with a clean and fun adventure any age could read! If it's not my year to fully immerse myself in the movies I once shared with my mother, at least I can look back over the year and say I authored a book instead. I wrote a book I think she'd be proud of.

This book was a complete labor of love. Each day when I would start working on the manuscript, I'd remind myself I was writing this book for Jesus and my momma. It helped me to channel things that maybe she'd like to see in a story. She loved all things Christmas, with every room in our house decorated to fit a theme. She might have had a paperback copy of *A Magical Christmas Wedding* on display, knowing her! She loved angels, and there's one that appears in the story! You'll meet him later.

I want to tell you why my main character's name is Mac. My mother insisted when I had a little girl, I call her Mac. She loved the character from her soap opera, *The Young and the Restless*. Since she named me from Morgan Fairchild's character in *Search for Tomorrow*, she felt the tradition needed to continue. I've lost four babies to be with the Lord through miscarriage, and maybe one is a little girl in Heaven with my mother right now, and she's named her Mac. Until that time, I've got my character Mackenzie Hart, because my mother was my heart and my best friend.

The Young and the Restless fans will also recognize Chancellor as well. Chancellor Mackenzie is actually named to celebrate our lovely little sweetheart in our family, my nephew. My niece named her son Chancellor after Mrs. Chancellor, who my mother also loved on the show. So, as you can see, another name showed up, fighting for the spotlight because my mother would've loved it.

My parents were married in 1955, so now you'll get that reference. My parents dated for a month and were married for 52 years. A love like that deserves a fictitious twist with a little bit of time travel added to it. And yes, my Granny did go to the wedding in curlers. My Aunt Shelby was a hoot and a half, and she's lovingly portrayed in the novel, along with the name of my dear Aunt Janice. I love being able to add family members to my fictional characters. They are forever named in my books, and I hope they know I love them. June was the month of my Daddy's birthday, so now you know where her character name came from. My Daddy's name was Bill. You'll meet him in the story, too. You'll also meet Jolly, in honor of my English bulldog, Rambo.

There are so many things I could tell you about this book that are personal to me and all the reasons why I love it but that would take another book. So, when you begin to read *A Magical Christmas Wedding*, I hope you keep your loved ones that you've lost close to your heart, put on some fuzzy socks, snuggle in pajamas, and disappear for a while in the world of Crystal Falls, North Carolina. Merry Christmas!

Blessings,

Jen Lowry

Heart Set

There was no time like the day at hand for Mackenzie Hart to finally try on her dress. The minute she agreed to marry Jordan the whirlwind of emotions and details bombarded her. It took one phone call to break the official news and the plans began. It was as if her mother had been waiting for this moment all of her life, and Mac couldn't help but smile thinking about her excitement.

Her parents knew before her. Jordan had asked them for her hand in marriage. She heard the retelling over that first phone call. From her mother crying tears of joy to her father admonishing Jordan with threats to not hurt his little girl, the talk of their life became all about the wedding. Her parents loved Jordan from day one, and she did, too. There was a way about him that sat well with her soul. Traditional. One thing among many she loved about him.

It had only been a week into the proposal and her mother arranged for a boutique appointment, carrying on about how long alterations could take and since the Christmas season was a time for weddings, if they didn't plan it now, they would lose the venue and musicians and caterers…

Her mother was right, yet again. As soon as the news traveled around Crystal Falls about the wedding, every local shop and business owner they knew wanted to pitch in and somehow be a part of the festivities. Especially since their mountain town always did up Christmas right, a wedding would be a joyous occasion that time of year. Mac knew it was the right time to say I do. Even if Mrs. Hart thought she was crazy trying to plan it in three months. It just felt right.

Mackenzie sighed as she parked in front of the tiny storefront down Main, and she rested her chin against the steering wheel to observe the liveliness of her little town. Construction workers lined up to pick up Bill's Hotdogs on their break. She watched as a couple of the guys were trying to balance snowballs on tops of their yellow hats. Their faces were soft with jesting at one another, fighting off the cold with a joke or two.

A mother was pushing her baby into Sara's hair salon, probably praying the little one would nap long enough for a shampoo. Sara's was the place where she'd find herself soon enough. Having your hair done at Sara's was a given. No other big city salons would do. When you went into Sara's, it was like walking into your family's den and settling in. She'd welcome anyone and everyone with a smile and a story. Sara had already met with Mac to decide on the perfect style for her hair. She knew without a doubt it would look lovely.

Mr. Thompson was rearranging the winter clearance sign in front of his hardware store. His movements were slow and deliberate, telling her his age was wearing more on him this year. She wondered what would happen to the store when he could no longer keep it up. He had no children to pass it along to, and it wasn't like the town was getting any bigger. Fond memories of eating Mickey Mouse ice cream in the store line while her daddy needed to pick up nails for a project momma had him doing on the weekends brought her to a smile.

More boards were going up on a downtown shop window, signaling another store went under and had to be vacated. More empty rooms reminding her that things change but not always for the good. It's not that Mac resented change, in fact, she loved how her life had changed over the past year. She didn't want to see the likes of a place she loved so much disappear or for change to mean she'd have to leave it.

Her mother rapped on the window. "Mac, are you coming?"

Janice Hart was dressed in pink, all the way down to her colored Keds. December days were bringing in cooler temperatures. She embraced her mom and immediately felt her warmth on the chill, brisk day. Her mother's kindness always spread through to her hands, so Mackenzie took hold of one as they walked down the sidewalk.

"What had you huddled up in the car? I saw that look on your face. Are you okay, honey?"

"I was just thinking about how much I love this place."

Her momma laughed. "What's got you thinking about all that when you should be thinking about lace or no lace tablecloths? We still have to do the final touches for the reception hall."

MacKenzie hadn't told her family but Jordan was applying for jobs in Raleigh and Charlotte, hoping to have them moved by the new year. He wanted the city life and the prospects of a higher-paid position in a towering skyscraper meant he could provide for his new wife and one day family.

He'd not had any luck with positions and secretly Mac was praying they'd stay in Crystal Falls. Mackenzie felt they could live fine right where they were. She already had a home she'd purchased from her Aunt Shelby when she moved to the beach in a retirement condo. It was a small house on a quiet street near the downtown district, but it was fine for them. There was always room for renovations, and her father was always working on one project or another. Adding her home to his list would have been a joy.

Jordan was still renting by the college, where he roomed with his best friend, Jake. Jake was waiting for his lease to be up, and he said he might head back to Connecticut. Being a small college town had its advantages because it could bring in students from all over the world. That's how she'd met Jordan. *If only they'd fall in love and stay,* thought Mackenzie. The town could have a future. But even with Jordan loving her, that wasn't enough for him to stay.

She knew Jordan wanted more than Crystal Falls, but she wondered if he knew that any place was just a place, a position on a map, with roads and businesses and people and traffic. As grandiose as the big city sounded to Jordan she knew without family and community and mountain trails they would miss out on the world. It was maybe because he was raised in D.C. that he wanted that type of living and what he called endless possibilities of things to do. The possibilities were not far away, but right where she stood. She didn't want to tell Jordan all of that. If he had dreams of big-time investment banking, who was she to stand in his way?

"Come on. Marjorie is probably pacing the floor. You know how she is on Sunday when the preacher is a tad late. Gets all in a tizzy waving her watch in the air like she's some timekeeper. Who does she think she is anyway?"

"Momma, be nice."

The bell jingled. Momma put on the sugar as their feet hit the green, velvety carpet. "Marjorie, dear. So glad you could fit us in with your busy schedule."

Mackenzie looked around. Other than their Crystal Falls Teen Miss pageant winner browsing through the new collection of sunburst yellow sequined dresses with her mom and sister, they were the only other customers in the store.

Mrs. Marjorie leaned in for cheek kisses and an elaborate twirl of Mackenzie, which made her feel like she was going on five.

"Janice, come on in. And look at Mackenzie. Your special day is here, darlin', and a fine day it is. Speaking of fine, where is that Jordan of yours today?"

"He doesn't get off at the bank until five, so I'm sure you won't be seeing him."

Her momma scolded her. "What do you mean, seeing him? There's no way he's stepping near this establishment. Text him right now, Mac. Let him know it's off-limits. It's bad luck to see the bride in her wedding dress. It means the end. Finished. Done."

"It's not that drastic, Momma. Besides, he doesn't even know we're here."

Mrs. Marjorie huffed as she held out two billowing dresses for Mrs. Hart to choose from, swishing them for full effect. The princess kind of dress, with high collared necklines and shoulder pads. The 1980s kind.

"Keeping secrets, are we? Well, that's not a good way to start off a marriage."

Mackenzie ignored the remark and tried to think of a nice way to say her momma wasn't going to prom, but to stand beside her as her best friend.

Her mother must have read her mind. "Maybe not so poofy. Something elegant. Straight."

Mrs. Marjorie answered, "We have all kinds, dear."

She came back out with fishtail designs that were tight everywhere but the flair. Clearly not for her or anyone else in Crystal Falls, or the entire state of North Carolina for sure.

Mrs. Hart stifled a laugh. "Do you have anything not so mermaid?"

Her mother tried to smooth over the awkwardness that had fallen over them all. "How about we look around a bit, Mac, while she brings out your dress for your final fitting. If I can't find one today, I still have time to drive over to the Chester mall."

Mrs. Marjorie came back around with a bundle of magazines in her arms. "And we have order options with free shipping. You can take these with you if you can't find anything you like today. But I've got something, I swear it or my name ain't Marjorie Black."

Mackenzie walked through the racks, trying to focus on the silk and the cut, the neckline, or the pearls but it all felt like a blur. She felt like she was still living in a dream.

She glanced over at the little sister looking up to her older one, swirling around with a teal sequined dress catching the light. Mackenzie smiled. She remembered looking up to brides in the past, as they walked down the aisle at church, imagining one day it might be her.

Three months flew by in a whirlwind. Now, she was in a shop with the loudest owner in history blasting over the pop music piped from old speakers looking at outdated dresses for her mother that seemed to step her back in time.

"Momma," Mackenzie whispered as her mom drew near. "Wonder why Mrs. Marjorie is stalling. Does she appear to be a little bit more frantic than normal?"

Mrs. Hart put up the dress she was holding and placed it on the spinning rack for later inspection. She was sure no one would come in anytime soon and need an emerald green ball gown.

"You might be right. Don't get me to starting about bad feelings. I've had a weird one all day that this day might not go as we had planned. Something told me we should've went into the city for your dress, but you wanted everything done here. Weddings at Christmas will get crazy, dear. Whose idea was that anyway?"

Mac grinned. Her momma should have known that from the get-go. Christmas was Mac's time of the year. Having the celebration of her lifetime right under twinkle lights would be a perfect backdrop. Besides, she had so loved Christmas that she even named her bulldog, Jolly and gave him nicknames like St. Nic and Santa Man, and Claus Paws and all the ways you name a dog without calling him Jolly.

Her mother continued, "Mac, I know you love Christmas, but do you realize all that goes into planning a wedding? We need to get this dress today and look at her with that guilt look trying to act all composed. I see it on her. Something happened. You need to be fitted. She's so busy worrying about the preacher and she needs to worry about her own time. That's my opinion. I'm just saying."

A voice called, and it was like Mrs. Marjorie was a ninja. Out of sight but never out of earshot. "I heard that. Guaranteed around here or your money back."

"We need her dress, Marj, not the money back." Her mother's voice lowered, "Are you okay?"

"I just remembered that I'm supposed to meet Jordan for dinner. I need to go get ready soon, and I don't want to run late."

She wasn't far from the truth of it. He texted her during her planning period, asking her to meet him later, but they hadn't made definite plans.

"As long as you're okay. You've got *the* look."

"What look?"

"The one that says you might be a tad bit overwhelmed at the moment. I've heard this story before."

"When?"

"From momma, years ago."

"Grandma June? What do you mean?"

Mrs. Marjorie interrupted, with the stack of catalogs and pushed them into Mackenzie's arms to help her mother decide. "I heard you had a hot date with Jordan. Where's he taking you?"

Mackenzie juggled the magazines about to topple at any minute. "It's a surprise."

"Always the gentleman. I know how anxious your momma is to get the show rolling."

Momma said, "Yep, it's time to move to round two tomorrow. The venue decorations are the next big thing to cross of the list. We're going to start decorating a day early so as to get a move on things. Start with the dress and it all works out in the end. That's just my opinion. The dress. Marjorie? Not my dress, but Mac's?"

Crystal Falls usually started to snow mid-November, so she would have a white wedding. Even though the weather appeared to be cool for the weekend, she was still crossing her fingers for a little bit of snow. Besides, who needed decorations when the magnificence of the falls in the background? That would be the perfect spot for a white wedding. She smiled thinking of the Billy Idol song, well, not that kind of wedding, but one all the same.

The park at the falls was where Jordan took her to propose to her. When her mother wanted to start booking the church and the banquet hall and get that ball rolling, Mac had to quickly put those plans to a halt. Jordan and her both agreed that the falls was where they wanted to speak their vows. It was the place where they first met, to their proposal, then to their marriage. Full circle in the very spot where she gave her heart to him.

Those were the simple, yet profound moments that changed her life forever. The ones she cherished. She was far from complicated or chaos or over the top, and Jordan was the same. After seeing her mother and Mrs. Marjorie huddled around the back door of the shop that led to her private sewing area, it didn't take long for Mac to realize that something was drastically wrong. Her mother's feelings were right, yet again. The feeling of discernment was strong with that one.

Her mother kept swatting at Mrs. Marjorie as if some assailant mosquito was in the way between them. Mrs. Marjorie disappeared in the back and reappeared with her dress bag in hand.

Tears brimmed her eyes. Mac knew it was serious now. "I'm so sorry, Mac. Scooter did it. Well, it was my fault. Scooter was with me when I was working on your dress, and he happened to spill my Merlot."

Scooter was Mrs. Marjorie's Siamese cat, never much liking the front of the store, so he found his domain best in the sewing room.

"Let me guess," said Mac, with a tight smile. "Did the wine land on my dress?"

She wailed, "It did with a splash, dear. It's ruined. I couldn't have the heart to call you. It happened late last night. There's nothing I can do, and with the wedding only two days away..." Her voice caught a sob, and she tried to gather her composure as to not cause a scene in the store. "Can we find a replacement here? Can you try on every single dress there is, and it's yours? Free. I told you we've got a money back guarantee, and I mean it from the bottom of my heart."

Mackenzie refused to allow a dress mishap to ruin her wedding. She saw the look of hurt wash over her mother's face as if she were devastated, and then she saw it turn more to anger than Mac had read in her mother's emotions in quite a long time. If Mac didn't take the high road on this one, she knew that it would sever a friendship. She needed to step in fast and make the best of the situation.

"Can I be honest to both of you, and you won't think I'm weird?"

Mrs. Hart put her arm around her. "Anything dear, just don't cry. I don't think my nerves can take it."

"I'm wearing the dress for a few hours. It's on and off. It's probably going into a box to stay hidden forever in my closet. The wine didn't ruin my wedding day, Mrs. Marjorie. It forces us to get a little more creative. I'll try on dresses, but maybe not tonight. Do you think we could set up an arrangement first thing in the morning, and you could maybe do an emergency alteration? Maybe no wine this time?"

Mrs. Marjorie put her hand over her heart, and Mac saw her sway slightly. "So, you aren't mad, honey? You aren't going to go all over town and tell the social media people that I destroyed your dreams and dashed them to smithereens?"

"No. It's only a dress, Marjorie. A dress that wasn't meant for me. That means greater things are in store. Getting married is about me and Jordan, even if we have last minute changes to our attire. Standing in front of God, my family, and friends and pledging my love to my man is what matters."

Mrs. Marjorie fanned her face, fighting back tears. Mac was glad she could relieve her of her worries. "You raised this one right, Janice. She's a doll. If it would have happened to Kathleen..."

Mrs. Hart laughed. "You'd be out of business for sure. Mac, you handled that better than me. I was about to fall apart any minute for you."

"Remember how much fun it was to go dress shopping the first time? You treated me like a princess that day, Mrs. Marjorie. Now, I get to relive it all over again. Tomorrow, Momma can get her dress, too. We can do this together."

"And I've had new shipments of wedding dresses come in since October that might find your fancy. The winter collection is divine. Your dream dress might be on these racks, even better than the first."

Mac didn't want to worry her one bit so she just smiled and agreed to a time they would try again. Her dream dress was in the back with stains on it. It was last years design and marked way down on the clearance rack, but perfect for Mac. Now, because of the mishap, she would be able to pick any dress without an outrageous cost attached to it. If Mac could turn it around, she could count it as a blessing. She would think of the positives only. She had learned long ago that was the better way to live.

Nothing was going to make her upset about marrying Jordan. All else was temporary. Except maybe moving away...that was permanent. Mackenzie pushed that out of her mind and hugged her mother goodbye and slid in the car. This time she put her head on the steering wheel and looked at the empty passenger seat.

The rest of this was supposed to be easy, or that's what she always thought. Right now, she wasn't so sure about that. It didn't feel the way she dreamed it would, and as she drove down the main street, she fought back the tears that wanted to rain on her, what did Mrs. Marjorie call it, her special day.

Mac couldn't shake the feeling that it was more than the dress that might go wrong. She couldn't figure out what was tugging at her heart, but she could feel something stirring within her. It was saying, "Change is coming. Be prepared."

Big News

Jordan checked his watch for the seventh time. No messages. She hadn't called or texted back, and it was so unlike her. He loved that she took time out of grading papers or reflecting on her lesson plans to give him a quick call on his drive home like clockwork. It was something he looked forward to each day. Listening to the sing-song quality of her voice was better than any music on his playlist.

But today, he couldn't reach her. She'd mentioned she was picking up her dress with her mother, so he knew that might take time. He had his own tailor appointment in the morning. Jordan knew her mother had been over-the-top excited and figured she would be as much as soon as the wedding weekend approached. On the night he asked her parents for permission, Mrs. Hart was already asking him about his family flying in from Washington, D.C. and where they would stay, and if there'd be any chance, he'd agree to her guest list without question.

He just wanted to marry Mac. Simple.

When he told Mac and Mrs. Hart that he'd be fine with whatever plans they made for the wedding, as long as he had Mac at the end of the day, that was what counted, he knew he made Mrs. Hart's day. Mac was her only child, and he marveled at the bond they had. If only he would have had that with his mother. He knew Mac was going to make an excellent mom herself one day, and they talked about starting a family soon after they were married.

He smiled thinking about what next Christmas could look like. They might have an infant to hold. His heart grew warm at the thought. So much to celebrate tonight, and Mac wasn't answering.

Mac deserved the world, and that's what he wanted to give to her. So much more than Crystal Falls was waiting for her, and she didn't know it. He knew how much the city could bring for them. Not only the arts, museums, restaurants, but great opportunities for his children to be involved. Jordan looked at the long term, and had been saving up all through college for a transitional move. He was proud of how he was carefully planning every single part of their future, thinking of not only their finances, but their lifestyle.

Ever since he met Mac, he felt like everything in his life was finally lining up the way it was meant to be. They'd met the summer before when he and Jake were out at the falls taking a run. It was like any other morning run. He woke up early each Saturday to get that time in with Jake, and they had their set routine. That day was magical. She had Jolly with her and was in full conversation. He looked for an earpiece and saw that she wasn't hooked to a Bluetooth like most people on the trail.

It was her and her dog. She was strikingly beautiful, and his heart caught when he saw her as they drew nearer. It was the kind of pretty that lends itself to feelings of intimidation at the thought of the approach, not sure if she was full of herself because she was so breathtaking or so humble that she didn't notice.

Thank God, Mac was the latter.

Jake must have read his expression and encouraged him. "It's been a long time since Jewel. Go ahead and say something. Anything."

Before Jordan could argue or even think of a line, he blurted out, "I'd love to know what he says back."

At first, Mac's nose crinkled, and she got this cute expression across her face as if she was trying to figure out what he meant. Her chestnut and honey wheat hair fell in loose curls around her and framed her delicate features. Her deep, emerald eyes narrowed and then, she got his reference, and her face turned a red liken to Tabasco.

Jake murmured, "She's hot," and for some reason, that word attached to the woman in front of him didn't fit. He was already feeling protective over her and ignored Jake, waiting for her reply.

He remembered how taken aback he was the first time she spoke. She had a country, sweet quality to the sound of her voice. He knew he could hold her and listen to her forever.

"I know it looks crazy that I talk away at him all day and night. He doesn't seem to mind or never talks back. The best kind of conversation. Jolly ol' Chap always agrees with me. It makes for a great relationship."

"What's his name? He's a cute one."

Jake laughed. "An English bulldog? Cute? Only to a mother."

She frowned. "Watch it. He's very self-conscious. His name is Jolly ol' Chap. Don't ask. I know. A little weird, right? I made him a birth certificate and framed it with his paw print in the corner. I'm maybe a little extra."

Jordan laughed, and he watched the way her eyes lit up. He stepped closer to Jolly.

Jordan put on his best British accent as he petted the dog. "I think he is a fine ol' chap, indeed."

Jake said, "Really? You're going to be that guy right now?"

"I'm Jordan McLaughlin."

She reached out her hand to take his, and in that very moment, when her soft fingers slid across his palm, he knew he loved her.

"Mackenzie Hart. But most people call me Mac."

Jordan didn't remember much after that. He didn't remember if he introduced Jake or did Jake stick around? It was a blur.

And they spoke every day after that. Signed, sealed, and delivered. His heart was hers from that very moment.

And now she would be his wife. He counted himself as the luckiest man alive.

Tonight, he would tell her about his job offer. He didn't want to break it to her on the phone. Maybe it was better that she didn't call him because he probably wouldn't have been able to hold in the great news. His salary skyrocketed in one email. Actually, tripled to what he was making in Crystal Falls at First Falls Bank as an account manager. Jake warned him it would be more hours, but he knew that was a sacrifice he would make to get ahead. He was young and had time to build his investment portfolio business to one-day branch off on his own. He would mentor and learn under the best in Charlotte, and one day advance to owning his own business.

Even though she hadn't responded earlier, he finally texted and left a voice message for her to meet him at Mariana's. Jordan pulled into their quant Italian restaurant in town and parked. Her car wasn't there. What was up with Mackenzie today? She must've been exhausted from teaching and was still taking a nap. He tried to text her one more time.

It was delivered but not read. Something wasn't right. He decided to stop by and check on her. He ran in and asked them could they move up his reservations another hour, and of course, there was room.

Something about using the word reservations made him think of another meaning. Was she second-guessing her decision? Was she avoiding him? He prayed not. One thing he wanted other than love was open communication between them. He knew that was his parents' downfall, and he wanted to do things differently. He thought Mac understood.

It's nothing, he thought to himself. *She's curled up in pajamas with Jolly and dozed off.* It was her last day before holiday break at the middle school, and he knew how exhausted she was from planning the wedding and teaching and directing the Christmas play at school. That's what he told himself to shake the strange feelings washing over him as he pulled out of Mariana's. It had to be that. It had nothing to do with him at all.

∞∞∞∞∞

Jolly was waiting for Mackenzie when she made it home. She gave him a quick hug and checked his food and water bowl. She had a stack of essays to grade on the American Revolution but she decided that her mind needed clearing before taking on her student's work. It was the last grade before the quarter ended, and she needed to put into their grade book, but her mind was so preoccupied she didn't know how good she would be at grading. It was the start of the holiday season, and she was sure her students weren't worried much about their grade at this point.

Besides, she had to get ready for Jordan to pick her up. All she wanted to do was snuggle up with Jolly for an afternoon nap, but she knew that would be impossible. Her mind wouldn't stop spinning. So much to do, and now with the new dress…
Nope. She refused to worry. *Lord, let me focus on what I can do.*

"It was kind of a disaster, Santa Man. But tomorrow is a day when the dress dilemma can be solved. There has to be something better waiting for me. It's all connected to a greater plan even if I can't see it yet. Maybe it will make more sense tomorrow."

Jolly turned his head sideways in that knowing look he gave her. She knew he understood her. That brought her comfort. She leaned her head against his and sighed.

"I love him, Jolly. That's got to be enough, right? We're going to get through this, right? And just because Jordan wants to move away doesn't mean we will. He has to find a job first, and maybe that wouldn't come so easy to him. No, Jolly. That's wrong. I shouldn't think this way."

She'd told Jolly all about her fear about leaving Crystal Falls behind, her family, her job, the town. Jolly listened without any words of wisdom to share, but at least he didn't go blabbing all over that very same town telling everyone she was having doubts. Because that's not what she would categorize them as. She didn't doubt her love for Jordan. She just needed to feel right about everything else.

He gave a soft whimper and padded up the stairs. He turned to her as if to beckon her on to follow him. "What's up, sweet dog o' mine?"

She took two steps at a time to the loft. Jolly stood by the hallway door. "What are you doing? What's this all about? You know that door has always been locked. Aunt Shelby probably kept her secrets in there, I'm telling you. Something we don't want to mess with might live behind that door."

Jolly's paw scraped the door frame. She thought the worst. Maybe a mouse or another animal somehow ended up in the closet and Jolly had sniffed it out. She grabbed her phone from her pocket and dialed Aunt Shelby. After their small talk that ended up being a long talk, she asked about the key.

"You don't want to go snooping around in that old closet. It's just tons of old junk in there, black widows, too. I would expect so."

She told her about Jolly. "Maybe I need to clean it out and make sure nothing got trapped in there. I don't want the smell lingering, if that's the case."

"Time, dear. Time gets trapped in there. That's all. Some say it's sweet but to others it can be bitter. It's all how you spent it that finds its way to one destination or the other. But if you want to see it for yourself, go right on ahead and move that armoire dresser in your room a tad because it's a heavy one. Don't throw out your back, you hear. You've got to jive in two days' time at the wedding. I'm looking forward to the dancing part myself. You think they'll be any single men hanging around?

Mac brought her back to their conversation. She had to do that a lot with Aunt Shelby. "Why am I moving the dresser, again?"

"Well, what did you call me for in the first place? Weren't you asking me where is the key to the closet? It's stuck behind the dresser with some duct tape."

"You duct-taped a key to the back of a cabinet? Aunt Shelby, really?"

"Really. Duct tape has many fine uses. Including holding keys for safekeeping. For people meant to find the time to discover what's in store. Keys aren't meant for everyone. Momma always told us to hide it safe for the perfect time. I guess this counts as that time. Good luck, my dear."

They said their goodbyes and Mac found the antique key with a gingham ribbon where Aunt Shelby said it would be. She pulled off the sticky tape and ran her finger over the tarnished silver.

"Well, Jolly ol' Chap, ol' boy, let's see what's behind the door."

She placed the key in the lock and felt a tingling sensation in her fingers. The electrifying wave pulsed up her arm, and it was like Monarchs took flight towards her heart longing for home as she turned the key.

Jolly sneezed as the dust escaped. The first thing that caught her eye was a palm-sized photo album with old black and white photos of her grandparents. She knew it was her Grandma June. There was a small portrait of who could have only been Aunt Shelby holding her mother, who wore a long white dress twice the length of her. This was a treasure closet, and Mac was in Heaven. Why hadn't she known about this? As much as she loved history, especially her own family lineage, and no one bothered to tell her? She wanted to call up Aunt Shelby again to ask her why, but decided they'd talk too long and she'd miss the adventure.

"So, that's what she meant about time being trapped behind the closet door. Jolly, what do you see in here? Or smell? What brought you here in the first place?"

Jolly shook his head, and then padded away. Maybe he was confused as to what led him to the door because he couldn't sniff out the culprit or he lost interest. Silly dog.

Mackenzie realized she could get lost in the stacks of papers and folders and old wooden boxes for days. She got that honest because she came from a long line of history teachers, and her current position at River Falls Middle was her favorite age group yet - fifth and sixth-graders. She would snap pictures of her closet finds later and create a new assignment for her students for the new year to write a narrative of what could be found in a locked away closet. She found a treasure trove of her family history so it seemed, and her heart felt full.

Mackenzie held a document in her hand from a top folder, yellowed with age. In the corner was scrawled with a pencil that was lucky to have made it over the course of time.

My Love & Dearest June ~~Montgomery~~ Harris (first time writing that is a charm),

I've got papers. This proves it.

September 3, 1955

This is the best day of our lives.

A date to seal it.

And now you have to deal with it.

Love Always,

Stan "Your Man" Harris

Her grandfather's writing was scrolled in beautiful penmanship in the corner of their marriage certificate. Mackenzie smiled at the inside joke of those quotations, "Your Man" that must have lived between her grandparents. She held the paper that started it all. So many stories about her grandparents, and she only had vague memories of Stan. She remembered his old green and white truck. She knew he took her fishing at the beach once, and he called her his good luck charm, Mac the magician, he liked to jest with her. That's all she could remember. She'd never had a chance to meet her grandmother June. She died months before she was born, and her mother was devastated with the loss. She kept her memory alive by telling Mac something new about June every day. It kept her with them.

Her momma told her once that her parents were so in love, up until their last moments together as husband and wife, that there might never be another love as pure as theirs. Mac felt she found that same kind of love with Jordan.

She knew that it could be that way between her and Jordan and was holding the proof that love like that existed with a marriage certificate and pictures of joy of a wedding day from long ago. Her parents were also proof of that kind of love, and even if Jordan didn't have the same models in his family, he was now becoming a part of hers. She put the creased paper back inside the top folder but left the pictures out to organize later in an album she'd give to her mother as a surprise gift.

Next came trinket boxes filled with clip-on earrings, Elvis Presley pins, and tassels meant for curtains. She held a pair of dainty pearl drop costume jewelry earrings and knew they would be perfect for her something old she needed for her wedding day.

There was a large box up top, dented on the side and scrolled in what could have been her grandmother's writing. It didn't match Stan "Your Man" Harris' handwriting. The words – *THE ONE* were in all capital letters.

When she tried to lift the white box, it caved more. Peeking inside, she caught her breath.

White taffeta. Lace of a beautiful design she'd never seen before in any shop or magazine or even imagined existed. Three cherub angels floated around a circle target with a heart in the middle, an arrow straight through the bullseye. She wondered if this was another inside symbol of her grandparent's love. Did cupid strike Grandpa or Grandma first? Why that pattern? Oh, she wished she were alive to ask her.

The advertisement paper was jagged, cut from a magazine and lying in the bottom of the box. The headline read, "The One." In such a cute jingle fashion the description said, "Needle nimble, needle thick, the wedding day is coming quick. Magic lives inside the thread and is heavenly stitched. It's for that lucky guy and his bride, to rush them to the altar and get hitched in the nick of time."

It listed the price for only one hundred dollars, and for 1955 standards, she knew that would be asking a lot. Today in Mrs. Marjorie's boutique, that price might have purchased a clip veil for her hair.

Her breath caught as she pulled out the gown and held it up to her. The flair skirt flowed all the way down to the floor and she imagined she could get away with wearing her white converses and no one would notice. The middle of the skirt was cut between the angel lace to reveal a layer of pristine silk. It felt like the river caressing her hand. The top had a sweeping neckline that would hug at the shoulders, with delicate sleeves of angel lace dancing all the way down to the cuffs.

This was the dress that was meant for Grandma June and now was meant for her. A dress made for a Christmas wedding. Her dress. Thanks to Jolly, her wedding dress dilemma had been solved. In fact, better than solved, better than she'd ever imagined. Forget the dress with stains. Forget a dress with an expensive price tag that would be given to her for free. She knew in her heart this was meant to be. It was the day for Mackenzie to find the gown of her dreams, and she didn't have to leave out of her front door.

Turn Back the Hands of Time

Mac said, "Now if only this thing will fit, Santa Man. Maybe no cookies for us until after the wedding."

She fumbled through the seams, and her heart sank when she couldn't find a size tag. She found the care instructions and smiled when she read aloud the tiny letters to Jolly, "Fall in love. Simple as that. Dry clean only. Magic may disappear in the wash."

She hugged the dress to her and said a prayer that she could shimmy shake into it. If not, she wondered if Mrs. Marjorie could make alterations to match. Maybe she could add a piece of lace or another layer of silk to the back might do the trick and with a long veil, no one would know the difference.

Jolly came up to stand beside her full-length mirror as if he were waiting. "Ok, I'll try. Don't laugh if it doesn't fit. I've got a plan."

She turned on Aunt Shelby's record player and positioned the needle on the seventh song, *I Only Have Eyes for You*. "I dedicate this song to you, Jingle Jolly. Don't tell Jordan."

Mac found her way into the dress and surprisingly enough, it seemed to mold right to her. As if it was made for her to wear it. Her grandmother shared her same size.

"Jolly! Look! How perfect is this! No alterations required, Mrs. Marjorie, thank you very much! Scooter, cheers to you, cat."

Jolly turned his head as if he didn't like the cat reference. "It's all because of you, Jolly. Without you pawing at that closet, I'd have never found the dress. You are a life saver and my champion. Merry Christmas to you, too."

To think she could have had access to her grandmother's vintage closet and that led her to wonder if there might be more in the attic she never explored. She had a new project for her and Jordan for the next weekend free from her honeymoon. An attic treasure hunt.

She stood in front of the mirror and bowed. "Well, what do you think, Jolly?"

Jolly sniffed and laid down, positioning his head on his paws.

"Does that mean I made you swoon?"

She put her hand to her heart as it began to flutter. The excitement of fitting into the perfect dress made her feel a little light-headed, and she found she needed to sit down on the side of the bed. Jolly stood up and found his way to her feet. Something wasn't right.

Where was her phone? Mac saw it on the side of the dresser and knew she needed to call Jordan. She tried to stand to reach out to grab it but felt her body falling forward. The room was spinning, and the last sounds she heard was the barking of Jolly mixed with the Flamingo's song, *As Time Goes By*.

She felt herself falling in lace, being wrapped up in it as if she were cocooned. The angels swirled around her from the patterns of the dress. She felt she was in the scene of a movie, and she followed the trail of the arrow released from one of the bows of an angel. It was coming towards her. The arrow struck but she felt no pain, and her world went black.

****

Jordan pulled up and sighed with relief. Mac's Jeep was parked in the driveway as he suspected. She was taking a nap or was lost in grading writing assignments or projects most afternoons, with time easily slipping away from her. He loved how much she dedicated her life to teaching. She sure had taught him about love.

He couldn't wait to tell her about Charlotte. They could move at her new term. The school system would be lucky to have her. He didn't worry about Mac finding a teaching job and was sure it would be an easy transition for her. Mac always was so positive about everything that came their way. This would be no different. He was sure she'd be to the moon with happiness.

He rang the doorbell first. When she didn't pick up her phone or come to the door, he went on in. He had a key for emergencies, and if she found out that she had missed their reservations to her favorite restaurant, then he knew she would count that as an emergency, for sure. He wanted to make tonight special, had a speech prepared and everything. The last night they'd dine alone as boyfriend and girlfriend. Tomorrow night they'd be surrounded by family and friends at their rehearsal dinner, and the day after that…she'd be his wife.

He called, "Mackenzie? Sweetie?"

Jolly was barking upstairs. "Jolly? It's me."

Jordan knew something was wrong when Jolly came barreling around the corner and continued to bark at the top of the staircase.

He took the steps by threes and stopped at her bedroom door. "Mackenzie?"

Jordan saw a crumpled white box on the floor and photographs and old papers scattered on the floor. He didn't see Mackenzie.

He called her phone again, and heard it vibrating, shaking on the dresser. She wouldn't have gone anywhere without her phone. Her purse was also by the bed on the floor and her keys were on the nightstand. Jordan went through the house and checked the backyard. Sometimes she liked to have afternoon tea by her butterfly garden he'd helped her design last spring. Even the winter drop didn't stop Mac from enjoying her backyard. She loved all things nature and said it brought her peace. Maybe she needed an escape from the world, and he expected to find her there, for sure.

But the backyard was empty and there was no sign she'd been out. Everything was locked up tight, and she was nowhere to be found.

Jordan did the first thing that came to mind. He called Mrs. Hart. "Is Mac with you?"

Mrs. Hart laughed. "If I told you what we've been up to today and how Mac handled it, then you'd be a pretty happy man right now. It shows the strength of that girl's character in the face of trouble, I tell you it does."

"Oh, thank God. She left her phone and purse here, so I just wanted to make sure she was okay."

Her mom said, "Wait? What do you mean? She left the bridal shop earlier to say she was meeting you for dinner. She didn't make it?"

"No. Mac's car is at her house, with her phone and purse. She didn't read any of my messages. Jolly won't stop barking. I think we need to call the cops."

"Oh, my God, no. I'm on my way. Stay put. Don't call just yet. I need to check something. If that's why Shelby called me, oh…I will get my sister."

"Hurry," was all Jordan could say.

Despite Mrs. Hart telling him not to report it, he couldn't help himself. His next call was to the Crystal Falls Police Department. Something wasn't right. He felt his eyes fill with tears, and he tried to block his mind from circling around all of how something could've gone wrong.

"Please, Mackenzie. Please be safe," he whispered as waited for them to pick up.

They reassured him they'd come over but they were sure she was fine. It was Crystal Falls, after all. He knew she wasn't home. Keys, purse, phone, Jeep…no Mackenzie. He waited on the porch with Jolly. Being inside made his heart heavier.

Mrs. Hart was the first to arrive, beating the cops. "Where's Mac?"

"I don't know," he cried.

She went in as if she didn't believe that he'd checked the whole house. A minute passed and she came back out holding a yellowed advertisement in her hand.

"It's happened. I thought it was a made-up story in our family that my momma liked to tell. It's really happened. I need to sit down."

They sat down on the glider rocker, and she passed a paper to Jordan. He read over the wedding dress advertisement and said, "What do you mean? Why are you showing me this? Where's Mac?"

"I think Mac found her wedding dress today."

His smile broke across his face like a NASCAR racer on the last turn vying for first after a long dry spell of losing. "Thank God. She didn't change her mind, then? Do you think it's this dress? Maybe she went to get it dry cleaned? That explains the old box on the floor. Maybe she walked down to Moe's. Let's call."

"Maybe she did. Or maybe she took a trip to meet my momma, June. More likely that's what has happened here. I need to call Shelby back."

"I'm sorry I'm not following this, Mrs. Hart. Hasn't your mother passed away?"

"Exactly, dear. If what I think has happened has actually taken place, I think that Mac has traveled back in time."

He laughed. "Are you serious? You've got to be kidding me. You realize you said that like it's a normal thing, right? Like that's a possibility. I'm going with the dry cleaners. That's the safest bet."

An unmarked police car slowly made its way down the street. Jordan looked to Mrs. Hart and shrugged. "I panicked. I couldn't help it. Mac's missing, bottom line. We've got to report it."

"But I think she's gone to a place we can't explain, and there's no way to tell the police what I know. They'd lock me away on suspicion of foul play with this kind of talk that I'm rehearsing to share with you."

"Is this talk about time travel, again?"

"Trust me, it happens. Let me deal with the police."

The officer pulled up. Jordan watched as she waved off Officer David and told him not to worry as soon as he was getting out of the car. She was sure she knew where Mac was. After a few more minutes of smiles and small talk, the officer left.

"Are you sure about this, Mrs. Hart. This sounds absolutely crazy. What if Mac's been taken? What if she's hurt?"

He felt like he was coming apart. Mac was the only thing that made sense. This was far from sense. This couldn't be happening.

Mrs. Hart turned to him with a smile. There was hope in her voice that didn't match Jordan's emotions. "I know she went back. It all makes sense now. Follow me. I've got to show you something. It's all Shelby's doing. I knew that women would be the one to spill the beans."

Jordan still didn't like any of this. Mac was not here. Plain and simple. His future mother-in-law wasn't sounding rational, and he thought he would lose his mind. He followed Mrs. Hart up the stairs and prayed, "Lord, keep Mac safe."

"He will, honey. He's in the past, present, and the future. There is nowhere that God can't be. Comes with being God, I guess."

"And you're telling me you think she went to meet your mother in the past?"

"That's exactly what I'm saying, and I have proof. Just wait."

She went to the hallway closet door and put her hand on the wood. "I'm going to get Shelby for telling Mac where that blessed key was hidden."

Mrs. Hart opened up the door and said, "Take all these boxes, and let's get started. There's one picture you have to see."

Jordan let her pile his arms high with half of the contents of the closet, and they settled in on the floor of Mac's bedroom.

She opened the first photo box. "Maybe it's in here."

Just then the phone rang and they both jumped. Mrs. Hart put it on speakerphone. "Shelby. What have you done? Why did you go telling Mac where Momma hid that key?"

"Because she was bound to find it sooner or later. It might as well have been today. It was her time to go, Janice. We all knew that it would be someday or the other before her wedding."

Jordan had only met Aunt Shelby a few times since she retired to the beach, but he got the rising suspicion that she was a little eccentric each time he was around her.

Jordan asked, "You believe this nonsense, too?"

"Honey, it ain't nonsense. We've heard this story since we were little girls. Momma wasn't the one to lie. You see any sign of the dress anywhere?"

"No, mam."

"I bet you don't. Because Mac is wearing it, in 1955. She's smack in the middle of the summer before our parents got married."

Mrs. Hart squealed. "I found it! Here it is."

She held out an old black and white square photograph. "Here's all the proof we'll ever need."

Jordan couldn't believe his eyes. This was happening.

Picture Perfect

"Turn dear. Turn. Don't stand there like a dolt. Move or get off the stage."

Mac looked down to see a stern-faced woman at the edge of a lighted platform stage barking orders to someone. Then, she realized the voice was directed towards her.

She looked down to see she was still in the dress and her white Converses. Mac made the turn at the end of the runway and tried to get her bearings about her.

She was not in her room anymore. Check.

There was no sign of Jolly. Check.

She was in some type of department store in the middle of fashion show. Check.

She was modeling her grandmother's wedding dress. Check.

The announcer said over a speaker system, "And for only one hundred dollars, the dress of your dreams. A magical, angelic dress that will put you at the altar just in time to say I do."

Mac made it to the end of the runway. She glanced out at the onlookers and saw how the young women were admiring the dress. It was stunning. She felt the same way. Now, she had to figure out what was happening. Mac turned and made her way back, feeling that this would account for one of the most awkward dreams of her life.

She went behind the curtain and bumped straight into the woman in the dark suit, with her box hat tilted to the side. "You almost ruined the show with that glazed look in your eyes. What in the world were you thinking about when you were at the end of the runway, standing there like a statue?"

"How did I get here?"

"Honey, I ask myself that question about five times a day. Now, go take that dress off, and let's go take our final modeling pictures."

Mac tried to smile but it wasn't working. "I don't know where my clothes are."

The lady scoffed. "Are you serious?"

Another model came bursting through the curtain, knocking Mac to the side. She fell against the racks of clothes and crashed through the makeshift curtain, landing square on the floor on top of the piles of clothes once hung on wire hangers for the models.

She heard the cameras clicking and was so embarrassed. A typical Mac move, even in a dream. Someone reached out and helped her up.

He grinned at her. "That's the way to steal the show and all the guy's hearts."

"And break my leg."

"That, too."

"I'm Stan. And you must be the girl of my dreams."

"Stan?" Mac pulled back and looked at her grandfather. It had to be him. She saw his handsome face moments before when she held the pictures in her hand, of him and his grandmother posing for wedding portraits. One by a three-tiered cake. Another of cake splattered all over his cheek. It was definitely her grandfather and she felt a rush of pure happiness. Grandpa.

Mac smiled. "Stan the man?"

He tipped his hat at her. "So, my reputation precedes me."

Mac laughed. "Something like that. I've heard a lot about you. I wish I could remember more. This really can't be happening."

"What? Angels falling out of the sky and landing in the middle of Ivey's Department Store? I believe it's the case. I'm looking at her."

"Stan, get back to work and stop harassing the models," said a short, stocky man in a gray suit.

He winked at her. "Yes, sir. I was helping a damsel in distress."

"She appears fine to me."

Stan laughed. "You said it. Not me."

"Second warning. Third, you're out of here, Stan."

Mac watched the exchange between her grandfather and the manager and took a moment to take in all of her surroundings.

She watched as her grandfather walked away, side stepping as if he owned the place and was as confident as a king. He had so much swagger in his step that she imagined he could be one of those debonair dancers from the old black and white movies…Wait. She was in a black and white movie but everything was color.

To have him here, a young version of him, right here made Mac's heart flutter. She watched intently as he added new sale signs to the suit racks in the men department. Why would her dream bring her to this place and time, and how could it feel so real?

It wasn't her time, that was for sure. The dresses. The hairstyles. No electronics. Families walked together, talking, holding hands, with no earbuds blocking conversations. The music through the store system was straight from Aunt Shelby's record collection. She was dreaming. That's it. Or she fell in her room and maybe hit her head? A concussion?

The woman was back and outraged, tripping over the piles of clothes and hangers scattered. Mackenzie and a couple of the other girls were frantically trying to get everything back to order. Cameras were still snapping away. She kept trying to get a glimpse of her grandfather. The world wasn't spinning anymore, and too much detail told her this couldn't be a dream.

The woman spoke through clenched teeth. "After you clean this up, I hope you know your modeling days in this town are over."

Mac said, "I'm really sorry. I didn't mean to ruin your show. Think of it this way, any publicity is good publicity. I'm sure this will be all over the newspaper."

She watched as the woman's lips twitched. "Maybe so. Maybe so. You better hope it...wait, look...someone is taking your picture, even now. My picture. Face right. Stand straight. Smile."

The woman grabbed her and forced a smile to appear on her face, which seemed to have a hard time making the upward motion with her lips. It looked more like a grimace than a smile, but Mac didn't want to bring that to her attention.

A reporter came up and asked, "Can I get your name, dear? We can add you to the lifestyles section. I'm sure Ivey's would appreciate the spread."

"Mrs. Sandra Matherson. M-a-t..."

"The model, first. What's your name?"

The woman huffed, obviously offended.

"Mackenzie Hart."

"Hart?"

"Yes, sir. From Crystal Falls."

"But I thought I knew all the Hart's. Do you know Victor and Jessica Hart?"

Before she could answer and say they were her other set of grandparents, on her father's side that she did know well, Mrs. Matherson started to rattle off about the summer sales for back to school and asked could there be a mention of the new fall line.

She moved away from Mrs. Matherson and back to the other girls who were each given an Ivey's bag. Inside was a change of clothes and matching jewelry for their payment for being in the fashion show, along with a two-dollar printed certificate for a free dinner at Bill's Place. That was a name she recognized. They were still selling hotdogs. Some things never changed, and they shouldn't. The hotdog chili counted as one of those things.

Mac followed the girls to the bathroom and locked herself in the stall to quickly change out of the wedding dress. She listened to the other girls' exciting chatter. It reminded her of her middle school students. The fashion show was the buzz. Each girl recounted their steps, the applause, and the opportunity to get a new outfit just in time for school starting back. Mac wasn't in December. She figured that out quick enough.

The girl that pushed her apologized when she made it outside of the bathroom. "I was so nervous. I really didn't mean to."

Mac said, "Oh, it's okay. It's no big deal. If I wouldn't have fallen, I might not have met my Grandpa."

The girl moved on, glancing back at her wondering what she was talking about. Mac realized that they might have seen her only talking to Stan. She needed to try to watch what she said. People would start to think she was crazy. Mac found herself aimlessly walking through the store, still holding the dress in her hands. That's when her luck had her run right into Mrs. Matherson again.

It appeared to pain the lady to admit it, but she came right out and said, "You were right. Any publicity is good publicity. I'm going to remember that. Mr. Ivey will be thrilled to hear of the free, front-page spread because of your mishap, and I might get a promotion. Keep the dress. You'll have a funny story to tell your children one day."

Mac folded the dress and put it in the bag. She wondered if this was the actual dress that her grandmother would wear on her wedding day to Stan. That she might wear with Jordan. One day. If she could figure out what was going on and make her way back to him.

Mac said, "Wake up."

Mrs. Matherson smiled, "Awe, how sweet. Do you feel like you're in a dream? I know that dress is fabulous and expensive, I might add. Magical, too, I hear. Or that's what they say."

"Who is they?"

"The makers, of course. Angelic Industries, down in Athens County. They've got their own rising business, and your gift is their hot market design for this year's running for wedding dress of the year."

Mackenzie said, "I'm getting married at Christmas."

"No wonder the dress chose you then. And now, you don't have to worry about what to wear. Provided to you free by Ivey's Department Store. Make sure you tell all the guests to come by and shop with us. Let them know you were gifted with this year's dress of the year."

Mackenzie frowned. "I wish I could but you guys go out of busi…"

She let the sentence drop. It was a dream. This wasn't real. Ivey's was not a part of her Crystal Falls. The classic department store closed before she was born and was taken over by a larger national chain.

Mrs. Matherson was called on the loud speaker to report to the office. "That's it. Mr. Ivey's already heard about the fashion show success and the newspaper photo shoot. It was all my idea, and I don't think I didn't have to fight for you ladies to have a spin on the runway. I'm sure this will be my moment. Sorry again for my snappy attitude. The pressure you know. Women in the workforce in a man's world can really add the strain to an already hectic life. You know the deal, or you will one day soon."

Mac wanted to tell her things would look up for her, to give it a few more years, but she didn't have the time. Mrs. Matherson rushed off, her heels clicking across the sparkling floor.

Mackenzie made her way out into the bright sunlight of the afternoon. It was Crystal Falls. But not. She recognized the landmarks and found her way to the closest park bench underneath a line of purple and fuchsia Crepe Myrtles.

A man and his little boy were sitting together reading the newspaper at the bench across from her. He was recounting the sports page to his son in dramatic flair as if he were a sportscaster, and they were discussing a player named Pee Wee Reese from the

Brooklyn Dodgers. Mackenzie hated to break up their lively conversation, but she knew that at least one of her questions would be answered from what he was holding in his hand.

"Excuse me, sir. Can I check the headlines?"

"Sure thing, miss," he said.

Her eyes scanned for the date.

Monday, August 1, 1955.

Dear Jordan

Mrs. Hart handed the black and white photograph to Jordan and said, "Look at the back first. Read my mom's handwriting."

"It says June and Mac, Summer '55. Best friends."

"That could be just a coincidence. You think this is our Mac?"

"Look at them together. That's my mom, June. That's Mac. There's no denying it. Look at your girl and tell me it isn't so."

Mac was standing with her arm around June. Her hair was pulled back in a ponytail with a light-colored bow. She looked so adorable in a flared dress and loafers. It would have made for a great Halloween costume. Her smile was as radiant as ever, and Jordan could feel her happiness through the photograph. It was his girl, but how did she get there?

Jordan folded out the newspaper clipping Mrs. Hart held out to him. It was a full-page report of a fashion show. He grinned when he saw a woman, who resembled Mac, sprawled out on the floor in a pile of women's clothes. She was clumsy like Mac.

"It does look like Mac."

"Seriously, Jordan? It is Mac. Read the article. Look at her name." She pointed to the article listing Mackenzie Hart as the model for Ivey's who made a crash landing. "Do you see the pictures?

Look there. That's my dad, Stan Harris. He worked at Ivey's part-time during the summer when he'd graduated from UNC. He's helping Mackenzie up, his granddaughter. Are you following me now?"

Jordan ran his hands through his hair, and leaned against the bed frame. He knew that Mackenzie would have loved being back in the past. She loved old black and white movies, the vintage clothes, and the music. He looked at her for a long time in the picture with June. She was stunning.

Mac might like the past more than the present, he thought. Wait, what was he thinking? None of this could be happening.

"This is crazy. You know that, right? People don't travel back in time. The magic wedding dress advertisement was just that – a way to sale a dress. A promotion. A gimmick."

"Imagine us growing up hearing the story. And one day we knew one of us would have a daughter, and we would name her Mackenzie because that was my Mom's wishes. It's a strange family you've stepped into Jordan, and I say that because it's true. Listening to my momma talk about meeting Mac and how her and daddy almost didn't make it, at first, I thought it was a made-up fairy tale. We never ventured into the locked closet until Momma passed away, and we found the closet key looking for all of her business papers that she instructed us we would find there after she was gone. There was more than the will in the closet. There was proof. All of this. We knew it was here but figured it was a big joke. It's no joke. Mac's back in time."

Jordan stood up and called out for Jolly. "I'm going to get Jolly his food and take him out."

Mrs. Hart said, "And I'm going to clean all of this up, and then head on home. I'll wait for Shelby, and maybe the two of us can piece together what we remember of the story."

"Don't worry about cleaning up. I'll take care of everything here. I'd like to go through the boxes in case I can find anything else that might help us make sense of all of this."

"Sure thing, Jordan. I think that's a great idea. You know I have to say that I'm so thankful you called me. It makes my heart glad to know you thought of me."

"Of course, Mrs. Hart. I know how close the two of you are, and if anyone would know where Mackenzie was, it was you. I never expected you to say she was in 1955. Are you sure about this?"

"As sure as the falls keep falling and rushing and flowing right down to the river and out to the sea. Call me Janice. Mom. Whichever one you like, dear. I know you're going to take good care of my daughter. I can feel how much you love her."

"She's my world. I'd do anything for her."

"Anything?"

"Yes, mam."

Jolly was already up and out of the back door.

"Would you go back for her if you could?"

"Yes. But how do you think her going back in time works?"

"Something to do with the dress, I think. It's all a mystery."

"Well, I don't think I saw a dress in that closet that would fit me."

She laughed, and a tired expression suddenly spread across her face. "No, dear. I don't think so. We know she goes back. This is true. We have proof of that. I just wish I knew how she made her way back home. Maybe Shelby remembers. For the life of me, I can't recall."

"She has to make it back, right? Please tell me she makes it back."

Mrs. Hart patted him on the arm. "Have faith, Jordan. There's a reason for all of this. The one thing I do remember is that my momma's story always had a happy ending."

"Then, let's count on that."

He walked Mrs. Hart to her car and saw her off. Jolly came back around the corner holding a ball in his teeth to play. "Not tonight, Jolly. Let's go see if we can find anything else that can give us a sign of how to get Mackenzie back."

Jolly dropped the ball and followed Jordan back inside. He was sure that Jolly was the smartest dog in history. He wished he would be the only dog in history that could hold a conversation and tell him everything he knew about what happened to Mackenzie. Jordan was sure Jolly witnessed it all.

"If only you could talk, ol' chap. She always said it would be in a British accent if you could. What happened to Mac, boy?"

Jordan switched on the lights in case she took a walk, but he knew it was wishful thinking. The town wasn't that big, and she would have made it home by now. He decided to call around to all of Mac's friends to see if maybe they came by to take her out for a coffee, or she went to the cleaners as he'd hoped earlier. His calls made more sense than the one Mrs. Hart made to Aunt Shelby. After he called everyone they knew and didn't get any news, he decided that he'd just wait at Mac's.

He called Jake in case Mac somehow made her way to their apartment. Jake hadn't heard from Mac, and he said he'd come over and wait with him if he wanted. He didn't want Jake around all of the "proof" that Mrs. Hart claimed showed Mac back in 1955. He wanted to study it all himself, by himself, without Jake questioning and doubting everything.

Jordan went back up to her room and saw the record player was still on. He walked over and read that she was listening to The Flamingos. The album was taking a rest. So, she was listening to love songs.

He looked down to Jolly. "Hope she was thinking about me."

Jolly gave him a look as if he was the only one for Mac but he'd let Jordan have a chance, and then went to his bed in the corner.

Jordan started it on the first song and let the record play. He sat down on the floor, in the middle of the pile of scattered objects, pictures, and papers. He took the lid off of the smashed dress box and read the advertisement again. He read the words magic thread and getting hitched in the nick of time. But it was some gimmicky pitch created by a company to sale a product. This could not be real.

Jordan was about facts. Numbers. Everything in his life made sense, until this very moment when he flipped the photograph over again. How could it be the summer of 1955. That number didn't make sense. None of this did, but he had the sinking feeling that it had to be Mac. There was no other woman like his Mac, and she was staring ahead of her, at whoever was snapping that picture, with that look of love in her eyes.

He started to go through all of the pictures to see if he could find any others that might give him some clues as to what had happened. He found some letters stuck down in an antique wooden jewelry box. They were folded neatly, and as soon as he saw the handwriting, he recognized it.

It was a letter from Mac.

And it was addressed to none other than him. Was this some huge hoax? Had Mrs. Hart planted it there when he wasn't looking? Was he on some reality show where they pranked the future bride and groom to be?

The letter was stuffed down in the box of other notes that were written by June and Stan. It was with the same stationery, butterflies and purple flowers framed the yellowed paper. This would've been some elaborate play, and to orchestrate this in such a small town, where no one could keep a secret? This was a good one.

Maybe he'd play along. He saw where some of the ink had smeared and knew that meant she had been crying when she wrote it or sprinkled water on it for full effect if this was a game. Let this be a prop in the play happening around him. He wished he had access to the script so it would tell him how to feel, what to say, and what he should do next.

Dear Jordan,

If you've found this letter it means that you don't know what happened to me. I don't really know how to tell you what happened. I do know I'm here in Crystal Falls but it's August 1, 1955. I'm here with June. June. My grandmother. Can you believe this? I don't know how to get back to you, my love. I'm praying that I'll blink my eyes and be back again. Maybe it was the dress? I can't walk around in a wedding dress all day. People think I act strange enough. I promise you I'll figure this out and get back to you. Somehow. I can't wait to marry you and be your wife. Wait for me. Please take care of Jolly. Promise me.

Love,

Mackenzie

Fortune Teller

There was a strange feeling of joy that filled Mac's heart as she walked down Main Street and witnessed her town alive with friendly smiles. The little town was bustling and in full swing for a Monday afternoon. It was definitely summer because the kids were out on bikes, and the convertible tops were down on the classic cars cruising down the street. Music blasted from cars. People were waving at one another with simple talk going on around her. Life was the way it should've been, and if she could bottle this up in a glass Coca-Cola and take it back with her to release it to the winds of her time to sway it this way, what a mighty fine day that would be.

She stood by a pharmacy window of a store nonexistent in her time and watched as a young teen served ice cream to a line of young children swiveling on checkered stools.

"Do you want a scoop? My treat? We're never too old for Charlie's ice cream."

She looked up into the kind eyes of a young woman that had the features of her mother. Could it be? The first people she would meet would be her grandparents. At least her dream was convenient.

"Let me guess. You're June, right."

"Yep. June Montgomery. How did you know that?"

"I'm from the future and knew it was you by your picture."

"Future, huh? Well, what ice cream will I pick?"

"You like mint chocolate the best," Mac said, with full confidence she was right. Her momma shared so many stories about her Grandmother June. She always wished she would've met her. The patch quilted stories were all she had. Mackenzie felt the sadness creeping in. Dreams weren't supposed to have this much emotion in them? Didn't they only last seconds? She was going on a full day.

Her grandmother laughed, breaking into her thoughts. "Well, who doesn't like mint chocolate? That's a given."

June grabbed Mac by the hand and pulled her inside to what Mac considered more of a teenage hangout instead of a place to pick up prescriptions. If only her chain pharmacy was this cool. Her students would have a place to go after school instead of home, locked in on video games.

There was a brightly colored jukebox in the corner blasting *Mr. Sandman.* A trio of young girls lined up, singing along as if they were on stage and giggling between lines.

June led her to a red and white aluminum table and said, "This is my spot. Jimmy will come over and get our order in a minute. Did you just move to town? You seemed like you didn't know your way around. Tell me everything about you. What college do you go to? I'm at NC State, with one more year to go."

Mac smiled. Her grandmother was an extrovert like her mother. She never met a stranger. Mac took on more of the traits of her dad. Quiet. Holding a history book in her hand or reading the latest news story on her phone. Her mom wanted the scoop and the story first hand, and most people were willing to tell them their whole story to her. She had that way. Mac thought her mother was exactly like June.

"I went to State, too. No, I'm not new. I'm Mackenzie Hart, but you can call me Mac. I'm a teacher at Crystal Falls Middle School."

She knew the history of her school, she should have. Crystal Falls Middle was around long before her and June. Her classroom hadn't had many renovations to prove that one. Not only did she attend fifth through eighth grade there, but she had taught there for the past two years, serving on the centennial committee to celebrate the anniversary. She was confident she could pull this cover and find a way to figure out what was going on.

"A teacher? Wow. Did you graduate already? You look like a student yourself. And that hair, though. Look at that style. It's to die for. I just love it. Is it naturally curly or did you roll it up last night? Sleeping on those curlers always gave me a headache."

She glimpsed at herself in the mirrors framing along the walls as June ordered for them. Mac decided she might need to twist her hair up so she didn't stand out.

"Do you happen to have a bow?"

"Sure, do." She reached into her small purse and handed her a band. Mac pulled her hair up into a ponytail. She hadn't worn one in years and smiled at the ridiculous situation she was in.

Before she could ask June more about her life, a loud voice booming interrupted their conversation along with the song playing. She hid her face in her hands. She knew it was Stan. He was singing, *That's Amore* by Dean Martin. His voice became louder as he made their way to the table.

June laughed. "Oh, Stan. Cut it out. You're such a show off."

He pointed to me, shaking his finger. "That amore right there caused me to get canned. Three strikes, and I was out. I couldn't work after I saw you. My whole career with Ivey's is down the tubes because of you. I think that means you should go out with me."

"Stan. She's older than us. Let her alone. She's a teacher."

"A teacher? How old are you, anyway?"

"Old enough to be your…"

Mackenzie let her voice trail. She looked to her grandparents and sat back. "I can't believe this is happening."

June looked at Stan. "She thinks she's from the future."

"Oh, really? Like my future wife?"

Mac said, "More like your future granddaughter," but was thankful the song change caught their attention, and they missed her words.

If this really happening to her, she'd need to tone it down because she'd read Ray Bradbury's, *A Sound of Thunder*. She didn't want to mess with time. She didn't understand what all of this meant, but maybe she shouldn't tell too much.

Maybe she should keep it all to herself for now. Especially with her grandparents. Something would have to reveal itself to her as to why this was happening, so she figured she might as well enjoy it while it lasted. She'd wake up and be right back in her room, with Jolly looking at her in his all-knowing way. Maybe this was a gift of an answered prayer she'd always secretly harbored.

Like how she always longed to know them, and here they were. Right in front of her, talking with one another as if there were no cares in the world.

June said, "Didn't you graduate, Stan?"

"Yep, with a business degree and now I'm back to settle down in Crystal Falls."

June frowned. "I have one more year at State."

Mac asked, "You're going to be a teacher, too, aren't you June?"

Just then, two mint ice creams arrived on cue and broke the awkwardness. Maybe her fortune-telling would need to stop. It was like she couldn't help herself. She knew too much. Oh, the responsibility and weight of it all.

Stan said, "Well, how about we go down to the falls later? We could meet up. I have a friend for you, June. His name is Sandy Cooper. You'd like him. He's not as ruggedly handsome as me, but that would be hard to find in this day and age."

Really, Stan. Really? Mackenzie thought as she wanted so desperately to put this smug man right in his place. Why the egotistical put on? Why lay it on so thick?

"No thanks," said June. "I'm busy."

"Busy? What will you be doing in Crystal Falls that means more than meeting up for a walk with two of the best guys in town?"

"I'll be hanging out with my new best friend. Can't you tell you interrupted a serious conversation about the future."

"Worrying about the future gets you nowhere in life. Live for the day, I say. Seize it. Conquer it, and all that jazz."

A couple of guys in lettermen jackets pulled Stan away. Mac found their cajoling to be hilarious. Spirited. Innocent. 1955'ish, and if that was a thing, she was witnessing it.

She'd always thought she was an old soul herself, more traditional in her values. She never felt she fit into the way of the modern world. That's why she always navigated towards history and majored in it. That's why she loved the past. This past. It was simple.

And now she was here, and nothing was simple. She wanted be with Jordan. Jolly. Her parents. Her town. She had to find a way back, but how?

"I want to see everything," she blurted out. Maybe she needed to move and keep moving.

June said, "Let's go, then. I'll take you on a tour of Crystal Falls since you're new in town. A new school year is coming soon. I have student teaching in an elementary school in Raleigh."

Mac asked, "Why don't you see if you can stick around Crystal Falls and teach here?"

June looked up. "Oh, wonder if they will let me do my internship here? I'll call them today to see. Why haven't I thought of that? Now that Stan…Well, never mind. Will you tell me more about your future?"

"If you promise me one thing. You won't think I'm crazy."

"I don't think you're crazy. Something tells me you're a little lost, but not crazy."

Mac said, "Lost could describe it, I guess. I hope I'm found."

"By who? Stan? Apparently, he must have some kind of crush on you by the way he keeps staring over here."

"Oh, no. I hope I'm found by Jordan, my fiancé."

"You have a fiancé? Oh, you must tell! I need to know everything. Is he here in Crystal Falls? Is he back at State? A fiancé? Seriously!" Mac caught how June turned to look at Stan again and recognized the look of love plastered all over her innocent face. "If only…"

Stan came up then. "I can read lips. I saw fiancé or was that finance? Not sure. I do know business. What's your business?"

"You saw right the first time, Stan," bossed June. "She's taken and off the market. Engaged. Bagged. Get lost."

"Well, then. June, that leaves the two of us. How about it? You want to meet at the falls later?"

Mac tried to hide her amusement as she witnessed him asking her grandmother out, but knew that wasn't really the way he should go about doing it.

"Are you kidding me, Stan. You? No way. Sorry. I told you I was busy."

Stan put his hand over his heart and acted wounded. He needed some lessons and quick. This wasn't high school anymore, but Stan seemed to not get the hint. Stan "the man" didn't really have the man part down. But who were they to talk? They were sitting in an ice cream parlor.

She remembered the date. August 1, 1955. What did the marriage certificate say? September. In one month, the two of them would be married. That seemed very unlikely to her. Especially with the way Stan was acting. Even if she could tell that June had feelings for him. Marriage was a stretch.

June grabbed her by the hand and they left the pharmacy behind. "Let's go to my house. It's not too far from here."

Mac wanted to say she knew the way but stepped a little slower beside her, taking it all in. She tried to open the door to the possibility of a romance between June and Stan.

She said, "Stan isn't too bad. He's a little immature, but at least he's cute."

June hugged her chest. "Oh, I know. I've loved him for years. Since I was five years old. Kindergarten to be exact. He kissed me under the art table in Mrs. Oxendine's class.

He probably doesn't even remember. I hit him. The teacher called my mom, and she laughed about it. She thought it was cute. I thought Stan was cute, and the rest is history."

I laughed. "You love him? Seriously?"

"Seriously."

"Well, why didn't you go out with him? I think he was really asking you to the falls." Mac tried to deflect to draw attention away from his fickle attitude and hoped she was right.

"More like he was trying to hook me up with someone else at the falls so he could flirt with you some more."

"Fiancé, remember. He knows the deal."

"Yeah, but it's a lost cause with me and Stan, anyway."

She looped her arm through Mac's and leaned on her shoulder. It was like they knew each other for years. Not just an hour ago, with a chance meeting on the street. It hit her that this was her grandmother. Her grandmother. She fought back the tears because how would she ever be able to explain why they were falling.

She remembered once seeing an image online of an empty park bench. The saying underneath the red painted bench asked, "If you could spend the day with someone from the past, who would it be?"

She always knew it would be June. Nothing like this felt like chance. Her feet were hitting pavement. It was hot. Sweat formed on her brow. Her grandmother's hair tickled her nose. This was real.

Mac said, "Why do you think it's a lost cause with Stan? I think he's perfect for you, really."

"Do you think so? Oh, going out with him really doesn't seem like an option. I'm moving back to State in two weeks, and he'll be here in Crystal Falls. He's too flighty to have a

long-distance relationship. Remember, I've known him since
I was five."

"Well, time can change things. Trust me on that."

"Maybe so. Come on. We're almost home."

Mac and June strolled down the quiet street. The street
had changed little in sixty years. She noticed a younger girl
sitting on the porch swing.

"That's my sweet baby sister, Margaret."

Mac remembered the story of how Margaret didn't live to
see her tenth birthday because she died of a lung infection
from polio. It made her heart hurt. She smiled at the child
who was holding a small book in her hand. Heidi. She loved
the classics.

"Who's this, June?"

"This is my new friend, Mackenzie. She's a new teacher
here at the middle school. We get to call her Mac. Isn't that
the best nickname?"

"Like you call me Mags."

"Yep, something like that."

She pulled a flower from a clay pot by the gate and
brought it to Margaret. "You can call me Mac for sure."

June sat beside her on the swing and patted a spot for
Mac to sit. "So, tell us about your fiancé. Jordan, right?"

"Yes, he's wonderful. I have a picture right here..." She
forgot. She didn't have her phone. She wouldn't have had a
signal anyway, and the thought made her laugh.

June said, "What's so funny?"

"Just never would have thought I would've missed my
phone. Wait until my students find out about this. I'll never
hear the end of it."

June said, "Oh, do you need to call Jordan? You can use
our phone. Come on inside."

June was already up and walking towards the door. She heard a lady call out from the kitchen. Her great grandmother wore an apron over a long, checkered patterned dress. She had a brilliant smile and eyes sparkling as if she were up to mischief. Kindness was written on her face plain as day. The recipe book, *Southern Best*, was laid out on the counter. She'd seen that book before, in her very cabinet.

If she could remember the way the kitchen looked, she would want this retro feel in a renovation project. If she could convince Jordan to stay.

"Mother, this is my friend, Mac. Mac, this is my mom, Violet Montgomery."

"Well, Miss Mary Mac, nice to meet you."

Mac was at a loss of words. Her mother would call her that on occasion. She wondered if June's mom knew her secret.

"She's new in town, and is starting a teaching job at the middle school."

"Oh, really? What do you teach, dear?"

"History."

"Well, isn't that lovely. There's nothing better than educating our youth about our past. I bet you're just filled with fun facts."

Mac smiled. "Like you wouldn't believe."

June said, "She needs to use our phone to call her fiancé."

It was funny how June kept repeating that word. Mac thought she heard it more today than she had her entire engagement. "It's ok. I don't think I'd be able to reach him. I could write him a letter."

She didn't know what possessed her to say that, but it came out. A letter? She hadn't written a letter in years, and never one to Jordan. Even that wouldn't make it, unless there was a magic postal service in Crystal Falls she was unaware of.

Violet said, "Letters are fun. Whatever happened to Margaret's pen pal? I've been wondering why we haven't received any letters back from her in a while. I hope she hasn't any bad health like…"

Her voice trailed, and Mac could feel the change in the atmosphere.

Mac tried to change the subject. "What are you making for dinner?"

"Oh, my famous meatloaf."

"It is famous," announced June. "Momma won the best ribbon at the Easter church bake-off."

"Oh, I wish we had those."

"Oh, you don't? Where do you happen to be from that doesn't have church bake-offs?"

"We do on television all the time, but as far as Crystal Falls goes, we don't have a lot of things anymore." Mackenzie realized she needed to be quiet. They had so much more. Like vaccines for polio.

"What channel has a bake-off? *ABC*? It sure would be a hit. I can guarantee that."

June said, "Call us when supper is ready, please. We'll be writing letters."

"Oh, you, too? Take your sister, Margaret."

"Of course, Momma. Come on, Margaret. Let's go write letters."

Her voice lifted in a sing-song reply, "To who? Let me guess? Stan?"

Violet said, "That Stan boy is back in town. I heard about him getting fired from Ivey's this morning. What future does that man have if he can't even hang up a tie?"

"He actually becomes a very successful car salesma…"

Mackenzie clapped her hand over her mouth. Not again. Lord, help her. This was harder than she imagined.

June laughed. "Mac here claims she's from the future."

"Oh, like one of those Hitchcock movies. I love me a good time travel movie. Have you read the new *A Sound of…*"

Mac finished her sentence. "*Thunder.* I love that short story."

"It's fabulous. How one misstep could change the course of history can get you thinking maybe going back in time might not be the best decision. Imagine us not having Eisenhower but Stevenson instead."

"No more talk of politics, Momma." June turned to her and smirked. "My momma could be right up there in Washington with the best of them."

"So, my love of history might have started with you."

"We all love history around here, dear. My grandfather was a famous anthropologist at Duke University. Professor Chancellor D. Mackenzie, a world traveler and collector of antiquities. We love our set of encyclopedias. If you ever want to check the out, they're in the den, dear."

Mac said, "I didn't know that we had an anthropologist in the family. That's awesome."

Mags leaned on her arm. "Awesome? Is that like groovy?"

Mac smiled. "Same word."

Margaret said, "I think it's awesomer. I'll start using it."

Mac wanted to correct her but thought better of it. Let it be awesomer all she liked.

June pulled them towards the stairs. "Let the writing letter games begin. I think I want to write a letter called dear my future fiancé."

Margaret skipped in front of them. "Oh, it's a game. I love games. I want to write to the future, too. That's what I'll do. Dear my awesomer future is how I'll address it."

Mac watched as she grabbed a handful of tissues from the hall table before they made their way upstairs. She sneezed in twos like Mac. Mags was a sweetheart, and Mac loved the relationship she had with June. It so reminded her of her mother and Aunt Shelby, two peas in a pod. Mac knew that her momma missed Shelby something awful since she moved to the beach, but all she'd have to do is call, and Shelby would come running. *Shelby should have been halfway across the state of North Carolina by now to arrive early for the wedding,* Mac thought.

Mags said, "I can't wait to find out my future, Mac. I want to be a grown up like you and June. It seems so much awesomer than being a kid."

Mac sighed and turned from June and Mags as they went about their gathering of letter writing supplies. She focused on how the very room she was sitting in had changed very little from her own time, and that brought her comfort if any could be had in the face of so much loss and pain. She wanted Mags to be a grown up, too, and she wanted to seal her grandmother in her heart forever. She prayed that both could come true.

What Next?

He flipped the paper over. Magic dresses. What if he were holding magic paper? He told Mrs. Hart he would do anything for Mackenzie, even if it meant they caught him foolishly scribbling on a piece of stationary.

He found one of her purple pens from her teaching bag, and sat down at her roll-top desk. Her Aunt Shelby left everything furbished for Mac. All she had to do was bring in her and Jolly and the place was hers. Since meeting Mac, they spent many trips to antique stores and malls, and flea market Saturdays were hands down her favorite. A few of the pieces were Mac's originals, but she had a blessing when Aunt Shelby pretty much gave away the whole house to her. She said Aunt Shelby was her favorite, which was funny, because she was her only Aunt.

Mac was his favorite. As much as Jake picked at him for following Mac around in all of his free time, there was no other place he'd rather be than holding her hand. And that's what he would write to her. He was no poet, but there was no better way to contact her that he could think of at the moment. If she could write a letter to him and it survive the test of time, maybe this one could happen to make it back to hers.

Dear Mackenzie,

I hope you know how much I love you. I couldn't believe I found your letter. If all of this is happening, then please tell me how I can find my way back to you. What was it that took you

He folded the letter and placed it back into the antique jewelry box, closing the lid with a prayer. Was it prayer that took her back? He wasn't a time travel expert, but the thought of someone being in this time and moving to another made him seriously think he was needing to see a doctor or a preacher one. How sure Mrs. Hart was about the situation surprised him. It was as if she knew without a doubt that Mac was there.

He looked at the clock and back down at the boxes in front of him. One thing he knew for sure. Mackenzie was still not home. He sat the antique box aside and started to go through the other items from the closet.

There were financial documents, house payment slips, and receipts from appliances bought at Sears. He respected the meticulous respect for numbers and figured he'd probably keep these same types of records.

Jake texted, worried about Mac. When he told him there was still no sign of her, there was no getting Jake to back off. Soon after he showed up with a pizza while Jordan was finishing up the contents of the third box.

Jake said, "Are you hungry?"

"I can't think of eating right now. Mac's in trouble."

"What do you mean? I thought you said Mrs. Hart knew where Mac was."

"She claims she does. But I haven't talked to Mac," he said. He looked over at the antique box. That wasn't a lie. Letters weren't officially talking.

His phone rang as if on cue, to break up not having to tell Jake what was going on. "No, Mrs. Hart." He paused and said, "I'm going to take this outside. Come on, Jolly. Time to go out."

Mrs. Hart had talked to Aunt Shelby, and she was crossing over the county line soon. It'd been a long drive for Aunt Shelby, and she was about to enter into a long night, Jordan predicted. He hoped they would get together and remember something. Anything that would explain this away. She caught him up to speed on all they'd talked about.

"So, the last thing you can remember is that Shelby said your mom and dad almost didn't get married? And it was because of Mac?"

"Apparently, my dad saw Mac and was smitten."

Jordan said, "Well, that's a little gross. Understandable, but gross."

"Exactly. So, what we can't remember is how Mac finds her way back home. We're still here. Me and Shelby. So, our parents still…well, you know. They are still together back in time. Who knows what time it is? I know during the summer of 1955 is when my parents were married. I don't know the exact date because my momma claimed that her entire summer was their anniversary. Some kind of joke between them."

He brought Jolly back in and ran back up to the boxes. He pulled out the wedding certificate from a folder. "Yes, here it is. The date says September 3rd, 1955."

He questioned whether or not he should tell Mrs. Hart about the letter. Maybe not. There were no questions answered from it, anyway. What good would it have done?

"Well, Shelby said to look for any more signs of Mac. Maybe from photographs or papers stuffed around. Mac is a smart girl. I'm sure she'll figure it out. Try not to worry about her, Jordan."

"How can you be so calm about this?"

"I guess because I somehow knew it would happen all of my life. One day my Mac would be a traveler. It was destined to be."

"And this still leaves me alone."

"Another way I know Mac is smart is her saying yes to you. She loves you, Jordan. She'll come back to you. I'm sure of it. That's why I'm not too worried."

"Well, I guess I can worry for the both of us."

"That will do you no good because it'll cloud your thinking. We need to keep our heads and hearts about us and pray for Mac's return."

He said, "I can do that."

She promised to let him know if she found out anything else.

Jake questioned as soon as he hung up. "What was that all about? Where's Mac?"

"She's visiting with her relatives. Something about wedding plans. It's all good."

"Well, then. Pizza time."

"You make it sound like you saved me some."

"I did. A couple of slices. See. I'm not that kind of friend."

Jordan grabbed a piece of Mariana's pepperoni pizza. He should've been sitting with Mac, enjoying a romantic dinner with her. He loved how they always sat side by side, never across from one another. She liked it that way because she said it was better that she be closer to him, that way it would be easier to hold his hand and steal a kiss on the cheek. He stole more kisses if they were counting.

"Don't we have some wedding plans we need to take care of? Like picking up our suits this weekend. Your father and your brother, Mark, are coming with us, right? Aren't we picking everything up together? I'm the best man. I'm just saying. I have to keep you up on these things."

"You're my best friend, Jake. Of course, you're my best man. There could be no one better I could think of to ask. You and Mark are sharing the honor."

He put on the fake tears. "I'm touched, man. I can't tell you how life-changing this is for me."

"For me, too."

"And then you'll be off to the bright lights of the queen city of Charlotte. Living the life. Come back to visit me when you finally get a weekend off, like maybe in a year."

"What about you, Jake? You make it sound like you aren't going anywhere."

"What about me?"

"Are you planning on staying in Crystal Falls for the rest of your life? I thought you were out when our lease was up?"

"I might stick around. This place grows on you. I'm thinking about going back for my master's degree. My dad keeps telling me it's better for me to get all of my education while I'm young and not tied down."

"Being in a relationship doesn't mean you're tied down, Jake. You make it sound painful. Restrictive."

"Isn't it? Look at you. Everything became Mac once you met her. You lost your freedom, man. I don't want to give that up yet. I'll focus on my education and career for a while, then maybe later I'll settle down. Who knows? Maybe I won't. Maybe I'll be a lifelong bachelor."

"I found my soul mate, Jake. One day I pray it happens for you, and then you'll understand what it's like. It's freedom."

"I've been thinking about my future a lot lately. Seems like it won't let me alone. It's time I start making some big decisions. Figuring out my next move. If I could go ahead and get that athletic training degree and work with the college, I might get hired on with their athletic department. I had such a great internship with them. I think it might be what I'm supposed to do. The future's been knocking in my head for a while. It's time I answer."

Jordan put his face in his hands and closed his eyes. "And the past is all I'm thinking about. I wish I could figure out a way to go back."

He held up the picture of Mac and June Montgomery. If only he could figure out how.

Mags took a piece of the printed stationary and began her letter without any thought. "I know exactly what I want to say to my future self. I'm going to be a teacher like you, June. Like you, too, Mac."

June said, "That's lovely, sweet sister. You'll make an excellent teacher. I've heard you instructing your dolls when you thought I wasn't listening. Literature appears to be your specialty."

"Maybe so," said Meg, with a blushing smile. "I want to live between the words. I can see myself teaching poetry. And maybe I'll even write a book, too. *Mags Goes to Candy Town* is what I would call it. It would be a special book about a little girl who gets all the sweets in the entire world."

Mac said, "Those are some great goals, Margaret."

Mags beamed. "I just have to figure out how to write it."

June sighed. "My goal is to figure out how to write my letter. I need courage."

Mac said, "How about prayer and honesty? That usually works. It worked for me."

"What do you mean?"

"I asked Jordan." Mac held out her hand and showed them her engagement ring. "You see how well it worked for me."

June gasped. "You mean you asked Jordan to marry you? But you can't do that."

"Well, I didn't ask him that, but I did ask him for my first date, and I even had to ask for my first kiss. Jordan was a complete gentleman and so nervous around me. It was adorable, truth be told about it."

"So, you asked a boy to take you out?"

"I asked a man to take me out. We went out to Mariana's, my favorite Italian restaurant, and afterward, we took a walk in the park. We kissed on the swings that very night, and I knew he would be mine forever."

"I don't know if I could do that with Stan?"

Margaret said, "What? Kiss him? He's cute, June. It reminds me of Bill Watson. I think I'm going to marry him, one day."

"Mags, you're a baby. What do you know about getting married?"

"I read, remember."

June rolled her eyes. "I want to kiss him. I don't think I could be so bold as to tell him how I feel."

Margaret said, "Then, use this." She passed her a pen and piece of butterfly stationary. "Write it in the letter. That'll be close enough."

"What do I say? I love you, Stan?"

Mackenzie said, "Yes. Say that. Tell him how you feel, June. Take a chance on love."

Mags passed a sheet of paper to Mackenzie, and she started her own letter. All three of them wrote in silence. Mac felt the tears begin to form when she looked over what she wrote to Jordan. This was different than a text. Seeing his name and Jolly's on the paper brought the aching devotion she felt for both of them to fresh light.

June noticed. "Are you okay, Mac?"

"I miss them."

"Who?"

"Jordan and my dog, Jolly ol' chap."

Mags got the awe sound in her voice that sounded so sweet, "Oh, I want a dog!"

"They're the best," Mac said. She pushed her tears aside.

June said, "Where did that purple color come from? Look! It's moving!"

Mackenzie turned the paper over and on the back, she watched as Jordan's handwriting scrawled across the paper. She sat it down on the bed between them.

Mags gasped, and her eyes widened with astonishment. "How can it do that? Is it a trick? It's like magic paper. Is this real?"

Mackenzie said, "It's real. That's Jordan's handwriting. I think he's writing me a letter in our time. Just like him to figure out a way."

June said, "I don't understand. Read it. What does it say?"

"He wants to know how to get me back."

June frowned. "Did you break up?"

"Oh, no. We're getting married in December, or I hope so anyway. It's only a couple of days away.

"You hope so? December is four months away."

"Not in my time. I was supposed to get fitted for my second dress in the morning."

Mags leaned in. "A second dress?"

"Long story. I bet my momma's worried sick about me. I bet Daddy has already called the cops and Jordan..."

Mackenzie let her voice trail. So many responsibilities and no answers as to why she was back in time, how she got there, or how she could get back. Besides the fact that she was missing Jordan and Jolly, so much was happening in a short amount of time. She couldn't let this happen to Jordan. She'd known he had been hurt before, and she promised him she would never do him wrong. This constituted as a wrong in her book. Would he forgive her? Would he understand?

Mags broke into her thoughts by squeezing her hand. "Whatever is happening, Mac, I promise it'll be ok."

"How can you be so sure?"

June was waving the paper in front of them. "How did that print appear on this stationary? I bought it at the Five and Dime. There's nothing about this paper that's trickery. I know what I saw. That just happened."

Mackenzie reread Jordan's words again. "Wonder if there's a way to bring him back here?"

Margaret asked, "Does he need a bus ticket?"

"If only it were that simple. He needs a time machine. Do you happen to have one of those anywhere in town?"

She passed the letter to June. No more secrets. Let her see it all. June read it and then her eyes widened. She laughed. She frowned. She flipped the paper from the front to the back, and read it aloud to an eager Mags who kept pulling on the hem of her dress, begging to be let in on what was so hysterical.

June said, "So, you really think you're from the future? And you think I'm your...I can't say it, Mac. It sounds so crazy."

Margaret giggled. "If she's your Granny, then I'm your..."

Mac said, "Great Aunt, it seems."

Mags danced around the room, her hair bopping to the rhythm of her happiness. "I knew I was cut out for greatness and at such a young age, too."

Mac had no clue what was right or wrong anymore. All she knew was that she was lost back in time, staring at her grandmother and great aunt. Wanting Jordan. Jolly. Her momma and daddy. Her wedding. Her life back.

"June, I'm your granddaughter from the future. I traveled back in time wearing your wedding dress. This dress."

She picked up the Ivey Department Store bag and let the dress fall on June's lap.

Margaret squealed. "This dress is so pretty. Oh, how awesomer."

"It's the one," said June. "Look."

June climbed across the bed and flipped over, pulling out a journal from under her bed. She pulled out the advertisement for the dress that she had cut and pressed in the pages of her journal. "This is my dream dress. The one that I prayed I could wear when I married Stan."

"You do wear it, June. You marry Stan."

Her eyes narrowed, and her hand came to her chest as if she were trying to catch it before it ran away. "Don't tease me, now. I just met you today."

"I've known you my whole life," said Mac. She thought that was the best way to say what needed to be said. She probably said more than she should have already.

Margaret rocked back and forth, shaking the bed. "Do you know me?"

Mac said, "Yes, I know you, Aunt Mags. It's very nice to meet you."

"It's nice to meet you, too," she said as she curtsied low with a giggle.

June shrugged. "So, you really want us to believe this?"

"Might as well," said Mac. "I don't know why I'm here, and can't explain a bit of it. All I do know is that I need to figure out a way to get back to my time. To my home. I live in this same house, you know."

"You do? Do we share bedrooms?"

Mac laughed. "I wish we shared closets. I love your style."

June blushed. "Do you want to have our very own fashion show? I heard the one today at Ivey's was a success. I see you were the one wearing the dress of my dreams."

Mac said, "It was a complete embarrassment. I fell through the racks and landed on the floor."

"Then, why not have a finale. We'll do our own fall fashion extravaganza. Let's dress up Mags first."

Mags clapped. "Really? This is the most awesomer day of my life."

June laughed. "Well, I feel really old right now. Thinking I'm a grandmother and all makes my bones ache. Let's see what this ol' grandma has in her closet that will fit the likes of Mags."

June styled both Margaret and Mackenzie in colors that she felt would compliment them. Mac felt like she was receiving a special beauty tutorial. When June's mother called them down to supper, they went with all new outfits, led by Mags, who pranced into the kitchen like she was the very own diva of the house.

She boasted, "Grandma June has arrived. Let the granny through. And you can address me as Mags the Great, if you don't mind."

Violet laughed at the scene. "What have you girls been up to?"

The man at the head of the table coughed. "Sounds girly to me. Too girly for my good." He then winked at Mags. "You do look great in pink, Mags. I've always said so."

"Thanks, Father dear. And Mags the Great, remember. That shall be my new name. I'm going to write a book one day for children called *Mags the Great*. I just decided."

He chuckled. "Yes, Mags the Great. Do whatever you please. How is my princess feeling today?"

"It's so awesomer, I can't even describe it." Then, she sniffled. That answered his question without her having to.

Her great-grandmother addressed them. "What have you girls been teaching Mags?"

"A fairytale," answered Mags, as she propped her tiny face into the palms of her hands. "One that I'm sure has a happy ending."

Mac sat down at her kitchen table, well, her family table, and was shocked that they all grabbed hands, including hers.

Her great-grandfather led them in prayer and with Mag's enthusiastic amen blasting in their ears, they all settled in for an entertaining dinner with Mags sharing her latest installment of the fairy tale she was living. It was all about a girl from the future who came to help a shy college student take a chance on love.

Was that why Mac traveled back? Or was something more going on behind the scenes? She knew June and Stan were destined to be or she wouldn't be around to see her wedding in any lifetime. She felt fine, so then what was it? What brought her back to 1955?

The melodies of her family rose and fell around her, and she felt it all at once. She was sitting at a table with those who had passed on before her, staring in their eyes, watching the way her great grandmother's crinkled in the corners. June had her mom's gentle way about her. The care she took over her little sister was heartwarming, reminding her of her momma and Shelby. And Mags…

She tried to hide her emotions behind her smile but caught Violet catching glimpses at her a time or two and with a look of growing curiosity. Maybe she knew a secret about this whole situation. She prayed she found out in time. Before her time ran out.

A Little Faith

Each thought that traveled through Jordan's mind when he tried to think of every possible way to go back to 1955 ended in the same conclusion. It was impossible. Whatever this was, he was convinced he didn't have the magic juice or touch or whatever it was that could transport him to Mac.

Without sounding like he was overzealous, he even contacted his college physics professor, Dr. Sue Triesh, to ask her did she think time travel was possible to begin with. She gave all of the theories of folds and wraps and he lost his train of thought around the third explanation of a higher-level lecture on quantum physics and time bending. Even if it were possible, it seemed pretty out there to him.

The doorbell rang, breaking into his sadness, and he jolted himself upright. Jolly didn't seem the least bit surprised that visitors would be at Mac's door this late, and he swiveled and pivoted back down on his dog bed.

Jordan took the steps two by two and saw that it was Mac's mother and her Aunt Shelby, wearing flannel pajamas, robes, and fuzzy slippers. A light snow was covering the steps, and the walkway glistened with the lights of the quaint lanterns lining the driveway.

"Heard anything," he asked as they burst through the door.

Mrs. Hart said, "No, honey. But we've got a piece of this puzzle that needs some reconciling and fast."

Aunt Shelby held out a photograph, then unwrapped her robe and hung it on the coat rack. "I don't recognize these people. I have absolutely no clue who this is. Now, how is it about to be up on Janice's mantle board without us having one inkling of an idea of this man and woman and five heads of kids. Things are getting weird, Jordan. Anything kookie over here?"

Jordan studied the picture and watched the exasperated looks pass between the two women. "Maybe they got lost in the folds."

Mrs. Hart said, "Laundry, dear? I could get lost in it, too, but I don't think that's what's happened here. Who are these people?"

Shelby was on the move, going between the rooms looking for any sign of out of sorts objects, new pictures, or something that would alert her of any strange occurrences at Mac's. Other than Mac not around, that's all that Jordan noticed.

Jordan decided not to answer them about the nonsense of time travel. He wouldn't have been able to explain Dr. Triesh's theories to begin with, and there was no use trying.

Jordan led them into the kitchen, and Aunt Shelby went straight to work putting on the kettle for coffee.

Mrs. Hart sighed. "Coffee at this hour? Shelby, you know we're going to stay up all night."

"Maybe we should so we can figure this out. This is Mac's business and our family's in a pickle, if you want to know the truth."

Mrs. Hart said, "What's the truth? That my daughter is a traveler? And Lord, her wedding is right around the corner. Poor Mac. I bet she's lost every bit of sense she's got."

"Poor Jordan," replied Shelby. "He's sitting right here looking like a puppy dog face a pouting, if I ever saw one."

Jordan crossed his arms and watched the play between the two ladies.

"Stop talking about Jordan. He's worried about Mac. I'm worried about Mac. There's no way this family could automatically appear in our lives, and we have no memories of them. How could we forget a family member or a set of them?"

Jordan picked up the picture in the silver gilded frame again. "Do you see a resemblance to anyone in your family? Maybe a clue?"

Mrs. Hart stirred in the caramel cream, her hands were shaking slightly, and the tingling of the noise of the silver spoon dinging against Mac's butterfly china cups from their last antique mall shopping day seemed to echo in the small, quaint kitchen. "What's

Mac doing to change the course of our family history? Does she realize the ramifications of one little iota of a wrong move?"

Shelby said, "If I went back in time, I wouldn't know what was wrong or right. I'd be a nervous wreck. I'd ruin the world. Ultimate disaster."

Mrs. Hart took a sip of the coffee. "I wouldn't want to go back, either. I'd be so scared that one wrong move would lead me to a new destiny. I love the life I've lived and wouldn't change a thing."

Shelby frowned. "Is that it?" Do you think Mac wants to change things? Was she unhappy?"

Jordan's heart hurt, but he didn't want to show it. Her words stung. Did her aunt automatically assume they were having problems and instead of marrying him, she ran off? That wasn't Mac. Mac was happy. He knew it. Right?

He ran his hands through his hair and tried to focus on the caring look Mrs. Hart was giving him. Maybe she could tell how much Shelby's words cut him. Jordan knew Shelby didn't mean anything by it. She might not have the best way of words about her, but he knew for sure she had a good heart.

Jordan said, "Mac is strong, and she's the smartest person I know. I'm sure she won't do anything that wasn't meant to be."

Mrs. Hart smiled. "So true. The Lord must surely have his hand in this. When there is no explanation with the human mind, I can then attest that He's still working it out for the good. Whoever this family is must be an important addition to ours."

Aunt Shelby picked up the box of dog treats on the counter and shook it like a maraca, dancing around the kitchen table. Jolly sauntered in as if on cue and put up his paw. Jordan felt the sadness wash over him again. Mac taught him to do that. He could see her, as if she were standing right before him, her shining eyes glistening with love for Jolly when he finally gave up his stubbornness and obeyed.

Mac was so many simple things. A smile on his long day made all the stress disappear. Her warm nature and kindness to everyone she met was so authentic, that it was her way. Her way was different than any other woman or person, for that matter, that he'd ever known. There was no getting around feeling good when he was around her, and when he wasn't, he'd get to thinking about all of the ways he could make her happy. There was no pretending with Mac, just being, and he loved that she accepted him for who he was. She had such a silly way she joked with him, but it always made him laugh.

Mac taught him about love.

Mrs. Hart squeezed his hand, and he met her gaze. "Let's go back through the closet, dear. We might have missed something grand in there."

Shelby sauntered through the doorway and up the stairs as if she was leading a dancing train. "Follow me, and let's see what secrets we can stir up and what trouble we can cause doing it."

"Maybe no trouble. A way out of this would be fine by me," said Jordan. "I want Mac back before…"

"Don't say it, Jordan. It's not too late. She loves you, and she'll come back to you."

"I pray so," he sighed. "My parents are arriving tomorrow for the wedding. It'll be a little strange for them not to meet their future daughter-in-law in town."

Shelby said, "We'll come up with something. No worries. No worries at all."

He muttered, "That's easier for you to say."

But Jordan knew they were worried, too. He could tell by the pensive looks on their faces, and they way they stole glances at one another was proof they had mixed feelings about this adventure Mac was on. Guilt washed over him as he made it to the landing of the stairs. He wasn't a strong praying man, and now he hoped more than ever that God had an ear for him.

"Dear Lord, I know I don't pray enough, but this time hear my prayer."

Mrs. Hart said, "Pray without ceasing, Jordan. Without ceasing. That's what Paul instructs us to do in the Bible. I'm walking stairs and praying. I'm kneeling down to squat on this floor with my old bones and praying. It's a silent commune with the Spirit of the Living God. I pray for Mac with every breath. God has to be working this out for good. I know this is beyond us so it's got to be all about Him. Have faith, Jordan."

"Faith? I'm praying for a little."

Aunt Shelby pulled another box from the closet, and handed it to Jordan. "Then, that's all you need. A little goes a long way with the Lord. Not only will he meet you halfway, but meet you right here, in this very room. Now, let's look for this mystery family in these boxes. Maybe we'll learn something new."

After dinner, Mags dragged them in front of the small television set. Mackenzie wondered how Mags would react to over one hundred and fifty channels, streaming services, and game systems. She would have loved to see her face at the surprise of how many things change in such a short amount of time.

June said, "Let me guess. *The $64.000 Question?*"

Mags laughed. "June. You're a know-it-all. It's the number one show. Why don't you apply to be a contestant?"

The doorbell rang, and Violet said, "Why don't you answer the door?"

June jumped up and asked, "Were we expecting anyone to call?"

Bruce huffed. "Better not be messing with my routine. It's my relaxing time after a tough day at the office. I don't want to deal with any hanky-panky tonight."

Mags giggled. "Father, I don't think you're using that word correctly in a sentence."

"Well, I don't think you saying awesomer every five seconds is right either."

Mackenzie leaned against the doorframe, keeping an eye on June and then turning back to witness the light banter in the den. What a day. June pulled open the door without looking through peepholes, window curtains, or asking who it was before opening, Mackenzie saw another way of how things were innocent back in the 1950s.

Mac could tell June was trying to hide the surprise in her voice. "Well, Stan. What are you doing on this side of town?"

"Hello, June. Is Mackenzie here?"

June turned to glance back at her, and she couldn't hide the crestfallen look covering her face.

Oh, June. I'm sorry.

Mackenzie flashed her engagement ring in the air, as if to remind Stan she was taken. "What's up, Stan?"

"I thought I could convince you girls to meet me down at the falls tomorrow. Since I am unemployed at the very moment, I need to fill up my time. I'm thinking you owe me."

Mac replied, "I don't think I can, Stan. I'm sorry."

"What harm could a hike do? Don't you ladies need your exercise?"

June said, "Maybe we could, Mac. It could be part of your tour of Crystal Falls."

Mac considered June's position. If Stan was actually hitting on her, and by the way that he was staring at her with those droopy eyes, she had a fear that was the case, it would be extremely awkward to navigate a hike, a stroll, or a tour.

But June wanted time with Stan, and maybe if they were together, Mac could try to play matchmaker between them. She could pull together all of her mental notes from every *Hallmark* romance movie she watched with her momma and mesh them all together for a super dating intervention.

She knew where to start. Honesty. "Stan, remember I'm getting married." She held up her ring. "If we go, it's not for you to get to know me better. We can only be friends. Period. I'm in love with Jordan."

"Got'cha. Just a tour. Besides, June is about to go back to NC State for her final year of college. We should hang out for old sake, don't you think? I actually would like to get to know June better, but I'm a little bashful. See, I think my cheeks are growing rosy."

Mac laughed. "You're far from shy, Stan. If you want to meet us, I have to check with June's schedule." It was time for June to make the call. To be bold and step up with some honesty. "I'll be right back. Stay here."

Mac turned and watched as June's face rushed with emotion. June rushed up the stairs without saying a word.

She looked back to Stan. "Stan, you know you need to stop flirting."

"Flirting? Me? Stan the Man? I'm trying to be friendly. I'm not flirting. Now, if you want me to show you how I flirt, I will. But I really want to talk with June." He glanced around as if he were afraid someone would hear his next line. "I'm not really good at these things."

"You need to be real, Stan. You can come off too strong. Can't you be Stan without the "Stan the Man" attitude. Just be you."

Stan's eyes furrowed, "I don't know what you mean?"

Mac sighed. No guy was a lost cause, not even her grandfather. If she were to get them married within one month's time, she would have to figure out a way to tone down Stan's goofiness long enough to get him to see what was going on right in front of his face.

Like June loving him.

June finally came back, and she had the letter in her hand. "Stan, I want you to do something for me."

Stan said, "What? Be me? Am I going to get the third degree from you, too?"

June looked between them and said, "No. I want you to step out on the porch, and I'm going to close the door."

"Ladies. You're both being a little rude here, don't you think? I came over to ask you a simple question."

"Well, I have a question for you, too, Stan. I can't ask it so I wrote it. Will you just go outside on the porch and read this?"

She passed the letter to him, holding on to his hand a little longer than necessary. Mac saw Stan's face soften.

"Do it already."

He raised his eyebrows. "And then what?"

"You'll know what to do next?"

Stan said, "I'll never understand women."

Bruce had apparently turned down the television set to be able to monitor the conversation in the entryway. He called out, "You never will son. Best do what June says, because she's always right. Just like her mother. Say yes dear, and that usually does the trick."

"I'll keep that in mind, Mr. Montgomery."

"You do that one simple step, and it'll take you far in life."

She heard Violet respond from the kitchen and it made her smile. "Yes, dear. That's why you say it? Really, Bruce. You say it because you know I'm always right, and that's the truth about that."

Bruce replied, "Yes, dear."

Stan said, "Will you just answer the question? Will you meet me at the falls tomorrow morning? Maybe around ten?"

"Will you just read the letter. Then, if you want me to meet you there, you'll ring this doorbell again, and let me know if it's still on."

"You're a little strange, June."

"Ok. I'll take that," she said. "As long as you know this now."

Mags yelled, "This whole family is strange. Wait 'til you find out all about Mac from the future."

Stan grinned. "That again? Futuristic fiancé' lady, tell me my fortune."

June said, "She isn't a fortune teller, she's a time traveler."

"Yeah, like I'm a car salesman."

Mac blurted out, "You're about to be. You're about to open the Chevy dealership and make your mark with an add of you and June on the back of a latest model, 1955 pickup truck piled with hay. Until you got the hives and turned splotchy all over, matching the candy apple red. The advertisers had a hay day with that one and it carried y'all for a while."

"Very funny," said June. "I see what you did there."

"You ladies are one strange bunch."

June pushed him through the door and ordered. "Read and ring, if you think it's right for you."

June leaned up against the door and sighed. "I did it. I just did that. Go look out the window, Mac. See if he's reading the letter."

Mags busted in. "Turn the porch light on. How is the man supposed to see all those sweet words of love?"

"Oh, stuff it, Mags." June flipped on the porch light quick, just in case.

"A hayride advertisement? Really?"

Mac laughed. "Really. It hits national attention, and it sets ol' Grandpa Stan on a sales hike with a nice Chevy bonus in his pocket. That's how you get your first..."

She let her voice trail. In the moment, she found herself being carried away in all she knew. Mac was one to always love a good story, and especially when it was about her family, she held on to every storytelling event around the kitchen table with fervor and eagerly took each little conversation to heart. She could write a book about a simple, small town life with a treasure of memories that make life extraordinary.

"You could write a book, Mags, about time traveling granddaughters. It would be fabulous."

Mags said, "I like it. You would be my protagonist, for sure. I might call it *A Magical Christmas Wedding*. You will have one, Mac. I promise you. You'll figure out how to travel back or travel forward, whichever way is the right way to say it."

Violet stepped into the entryway, wiping her bubble coated hands on a rooster patterned towel. "The house is too small not to overhear every little tidbit of information around here. If you're a traveler, Mac, then you aren't the only one. Follow me."

June said, "I want to wait to see if Stan reads my letter."

Mac said, "I know he will."

"Do you know the story of that, too? Did you know we would write letters? And that Stan would come tonight?"

"No, I didn't know any of that. I do know the ending, and it'll work out okay." She hoped so, anyway. With her being here, did she mess up the balance of the world as she knew it?

Mags said, "I'm proud of you, June. You talked to that handsome ol' grandpa and pushed him out the door. Impressive. Where did you get that boldness from?"

"Mac."

"What did I do?"

"If you can travel back in time and not fall apart in a million pieces, then I can hand Stan a love letter and slam a door in his face."

"Well, he did tell me a secret when you walked away. He said he wasn't too good at the talking to girls thing, so that's why he wanted me to tag along tomorrow. That alone lets me know he does like you."

June said, "It wasn't *War and Peace*. It wouldn't have taken him this long to go through my letter and make a decision. He read it and left, Mac. He didn't ring the bell."

Mags said, "Let me check. I bet he's out there rereading it for the third time, in disbelief that an actual girl fell for him. Especially a girl like you, June. You're a catch if I ever saw one."

Mags swung open the door and stepped on the porch. Mackenzie watched her face turn pensive. Then, her eyes furrowed and she turned her head every which way. No sign of him. June was right. Stan was gone.

Violet said, "Well, don't despair, dear. There are so many fishes in the sea."

Bruce said, "I don't like being compared to a fish. Am I a swordfish or a tuna? You better not say a minnow. I mean, why do people say that phrase about being more fish in the sea. I don't see no women fisherman out there rocking boats with slickers on battling waves. It's beyond me."

Violet smirked. "I'm going to rock your boat, if you aren't careful, Bruce. Leave your father to the gameshow, and we need to head on up to the mystical closet."

"Not that again," joked Bruce.

"Well, I know it's true. And Mac might confirm it. My family is quite a special one, if you disagree on that Bruce, we'll talk later."

Bruce smiled. "Yes, dear. You and my girls are special, indeed. And I'm awesomer to be a part of this house."

Mags said, "I do think that sounds a little strange to my ears now that I hear Father say it."

"It's awesome. That's all. Short and sweet."

June sighed, squaring her shoulders. "Just like you, Mags."

Violet led them to the closet. It seemed so far away the moment that Jolly took her to the closet, scratching on the door.

"It's in here that holds the secrets to the family."

June said, "Why haven't you ever told us about this, Mother?"

"Well, it's not like you go around telling your daughters about travelers."

"You call them travelers. Is that the term?"

"Well, if we are out at the *Five and Dime* and happen to mention our Mac here, it's easier to cover up she's a traveler. If we stick the word time in front of it, don't you think it takes on a whole new meaning of suspicion? Now, Mac. I think you should open the closet. Stand right here and let me get the key."

"Let me guess. You keep it taped to the back of the armoire?"

Violet smiled. "Not in this lifetime. Under the mattress. I saw it in a movie once. Seemed like a great hiding place to me."

June said, "If I have these traveler abilities, let me go back in time and never give Stan the letter."

Violet returned holding out the key to Mac. "What was in the letter anyway?"

Mags reported as if it were breaking news. "And now in Crystal Falls, where a girl falls madly in love with a jerk, and he doesn't ring her bell."

Violet said, "Oh, I see. A love letter? And you did this because you couldn't tell him and you wanted him to know before going back to State?"

"Something like that."

"Well, your senior year will be filled with fun memories that will last you a lifetime. Games. After parties at The Packhouse Diner, and then meeting your little ones in student teaching. It'll be so busy you'll forget all about Stan."

June said, "Hopefully."

Mac gave her a quick squeeze, and then slowly turned the key in the lock. The door latch made a popping sound. The expectation for what was behind the door was palpable. She held her breath as she creaked open the door. Would a secret be revealed inside that would help her find her way back home? She prayed that it would be so, because her wedding was fast approaching, and she wanted to make it back in time before Jordan even realized she was gone.

No Laughing Matter

The old contents from the closet lined up on the floor around Jordan, Mrs. Hart, and Aunt Shelby. He opened up a rectangular box in front of him with strange symbols and writings on the side, and took out a gentleman's hat.

Aunt Shelby whistled. "Look at that tweed twilby. This had to belong to our Chancellor because I remember this in pictures. He'd always stand with his hand in his pocket, and a pocket watch fob would hang from his coat. Don't you remember those pictures, Janice. Let's look for them. Amazing the hat looks practically brand new. It doesn't even have that musty old smell."

Jordan pulled the hat away from Aunt Shelby's nose and noticed the way Mrs. Hart's hand was shaking as she was going through her own stack of memories. She was trying to appear strong, but he could see through her resolve.

"You're telling me about faith, Mrs. Hart. I think we might need to stop and pray together. I'm feeling we both could use a little."

Mrs. Hart put down the collection of pictures and took Jordan's hand. "That's a mighty fine idea, if I ever heard of one. Lead us, dear."

"Well, I don't really know how to pray out loud. Usually that's Mac's job."

"Rubbish," barked Aunt Shelby, startling them. "Anyone and their momma can pray out loud."

Jordan said, "It's not always that easy, Aunt Shelby. What if I don't know what to say?"

"The Holy Spirit already knows what the deal is. You're petitioning to God. Saying what is on your heart is about enough anyone can do when they are talking to the good Lord above. There is no right or wrong way to say it. Jesus did tell us it didn't need to be loud and long. We could get into our closet to pray, and that would be fine with the Lord."

"Maybe that's it. Maybe I need to get into the closet. That might work."

Mrs. Hart said, "I don't think Jesus meant literally get into the hallway closet, dear. I think it meant that you could pray between you and the Lord, and the petitions would be heard. It's not always about having to pray in church, you know?"

Jordan fit the hat on his head, pushing it down over his thick curls. He winked at the ladies, feeling this newfound hope swell within him, as if he could feel the well of faith begin to build. "Well, what if you guys stuff me in the closet, anyway. I have to try."

"Are you trying to tell me you think I had a magic house? That this closet would be some portal? Look at the way Mac left her bedroom. Do you think she would have climbed into the closet? I doubt that very much, young Jordan. Sweet, cute, definitely cute, but your light's not coming on up there in your attic."

Jordan smiled. "But the light might come on in the closet." Jordan patted Jolly on the head and gave him a good look in the eye. "You take care of Mrs. Hart and Aunt Shelby until I get back home. I'm going to bring your momma back."

Mrs. Hart said, "I actually think Shelby is right on this one."

"I'm right on a lot more than you give me credit for, sis."

Mrs. Hart continued without giving Aunt Shelby an audience, "You sound like you think if we pack you into the closet like a sardine and you pray, you'll just disappear and go back to 1955? Do you know how ludicrous that sounds?"

Jordan laughed. "Weren't y'all the ones telling me about Mac time traveling and showing me all these pictures of Mac back with June? If that can be, why can't this be?"

Aunt Shelby said, "Well, our momma never told us about you? I'm sure that would have been a dramatic memory of you showing up like a knight to save the princess. She wouldn't have forgotten you, Jordan."

Jordan was still hopeful. "She might've never had the chance to meet me. I'm sure there are many unknowns in this scenario, and this might be one of them. Maybe I'll go flip and grab Mac's hand, and we make it right back before a blink of an eye. Besides, she might not have remembered me."

"Oh, she would've remembered you all right," said Aunt Shelby. "It's not like there were many mixed couples back in 1955. It might not be a good idea for you to do this, Jordan. Times were different. People..." she trailed off and a sadness washed over her face. "They might not understand. I think we need to pray to keep you here, and bring Mac back."

"I think you shouldn't worry about me. I can take care of myself. Let me worry about me. I'm worrying about Mac."

Mrs. Hart said, "I'll admit it. I'm scared out of my mind. And now, if you do this, it'll make my worry double."

He squeezed Mrs. Hart's hand. Her trembling had not subsided. "I can see that your strong resolve at first seems to be crumbling. That means that you might have a mother's intuition that something is happening to Mac. I have to try. I'll do whatever I can to make sure Mac's safe."

"It's not that. I have no doubt my family takes care of Mac. We don't know who this family is and they somehow belong to us or they wouldn't have shown up on my mantle. What else is Mac messing with back in time? If a family appears, does that mean someone else disappears? Maybe even Mac?"

Jordan was all about the facts. "Don't think of these what ifs. I need you to focus on what we know, and let's keep digging. Let me try the closet."

Aunt Shelby stood up first and was already making her way into the hall. "The Lord does tell us prayer can move mountains."

Mrs. Hart couldn't hide the worry in her voice. "Time is the mountain we're facing, and I have a sinking feeling lives depend on it."

Jordan opened the closet and looked to the space under the shelves. He figured he could fit himself into the tight space by pulling his legs up like he was practicing for a fire drill in elementary school.

Aunt Shelby said, "You need a shrink machine and a time machine."

"Funny," he said. "You got one?"

"It must be this closet," Mrs. Hart answered. "There's no other explanation. I'm going to not fight you on this Jordan but pray instead."

Jordan sneezed as he huddled in. When he fit inside, his thoughts went to the ordinary. Nothing was unusual about the closet. His doubt crept in. "It's musty and old. I've got a feeling it might be more than the closet. That Mac is special. I know she's special, but some kind of special. You know what I mean?"

Mrs. Hart said, "So, if you think it's Mac, then why are you stuffed down there looking like a packed sardine?"

"Because I'll do anything to get Mac back. I can't risk the thought of losing her. She's my world, Mrs. Hart. Without Mac..."

His voice trailed, and he felt his throat begin to swell with his emotion. Mac was everything. He bowed his head between his knees and positioned the hat further on his head.

His voice was muffled, and he tried to hide his fears by covering his face. "Can you please shut the door on me, Mrs. Hart?"

"You're one foolish boy, but I love you for it. You love my Mac, and I don't think you'll ever do her wrong."

"Not a chance. Take care of Jolly until we both get back."

He said it with a confidence he didn't feel. The door closed, and the darkness engulfed him. His heart pattered against his knee. He heard the thud, thud, thud in its quick rhythmic pattern. Everything before today made sense. Now it was all upside down.

"Lord," he called, "I don't have a power within me to change this. You do. Fix it, Lord. Whatever this is, and wherever Mac is, let me get to her or bring her home to me. Somehow fix it."

That's when he heard it. A whisper soft against his neck, with the hairs standing straight up as in salute to the power behind it.

"That's what I'm doing."

Surprise Visit

Violet said as she pushed open the door, "Sometimes secrets are better kept locked away. Other times we should let the secret live between two people. Travelers share a secret that others can't understand. It's a language unique to a traveler. My mother called it a mission possible, when all things appear impossible, a traveler can help heal all."

June asked, "Who else is a traveler in our family?"

"My grandfather Chancellor was a famous world traveler. I'll show you all of the documentation we have on him."

Violet began to lift the boxes. Some were the very ones that Mac recognized from her own treasure hunt.

Mac pointed to the top shelf. "My journey started at this very closet. This is where I found your dress, June."

"My dress," she sighed. "Not for the one that ran away tonight too chicken to ring a bell."

"It'll happen, June. I'm still here. We're going to the falls tomorrow, for sure. I'm turning in my ticket for a tour."

"Can I go," begged Mags.

"No, you're just getting over that nasty cold. You'll have to hear all about the adventure when they get home. We'll let them take over the den and do a retelling."

June said, "Momma, you're always so dramatic."

"I live vicariously through my girls. Now, let's learn all about my grandfather."

"You called?"

Violet screamed. "Bruce. We have a stranger in our house."

"I'm no stranger. I've already spoken to your husband. A nice fellow, if I must say. I'm Chancellor. Instead of going through dusty boxes, you should ask me yourself."

"My mother spoke of your ways. We have us a new traveler in town. This is Mackenzie."

She was going to believe this was happening. It was an answered prayer. She had answers, and he could help her solve them. "Mackenzie Hart. It's nice to meet you."

"Are you on your first trip or is this one of many?"

"My first."

"You've got the fresh look about you. You'll get the swing of things, I'm sure of it."

"And you've traveled a lot?"

"I kept a journal once. I tried to pass it off as a science fiction novel, like H.G. Wells. He pulled it off well, as his name suggests. Me, I lost it once and never recovered it. So, I lost count. I've been traveling awhile, if you must know."

"And how do I get back to my time?"

"You go when you're ready to go."

Mags pouted. "I want her to stay."

"She'll stay until it's time to go, and then she'll be on her way to carry out her own life. Right now, everything in her world is almost at a standstill. They're waiting. When you return, you'll step back into your life as if you've never been away."

"So, why did I come back?"

"You have a purpose here, Mac. I can't tell you what that is. You'll know deep down in your spirit. You'll figure it all out or you'll continue to stay until you do. Try not to get too comfortable. I did that once and lost track of time."

"I can't do that. I have Jordan waiting for me. We're to be married in two days."

"Then, your mission possible needs to possibly hurry it up a little. Put it on fast speed. Pray. Connect to whatever it is that brought you here and get the ball rolling."

"You make it sound so simple."

"It is when it's right."

"But how do I know when it's...

And before she could ask him the next question, he was gone again. The papers on the floor did a little shiver dance as the wind stirred up in the room. Violet, June, and Mags were all holding hands, leaning forward as if they had just witnessed a miracle. In fact, they had.

Mac stared at them and shrugged. "Well, now I have no clue what to do."

Violet patted her arm. "Go to the falls in the morning. Maybe you're here for June, after all. June, go get the curlers. Let me roll your hair. We're getting you ready for a morning date. Mags, go pick out a lucky dress. If it comes from Mags the Great then it's fitting to fetch a guy."

Mags saluted. "I'm on my mission."

"A mission?" asked Mac, staring at Violet, wishing that it all would start to make sense.

"A mission possible, my mother always said. It's possible with the Lord. That's why you're here. An agent for His doing, so I have no fear it'll work out just fine."

"I wish I had your resolve."

Mags came back in swishing a black and white checkered dress and a bag of pink rollers. "What we do for men."

"What do you know about it," asked Violet.

"I read, remember."

"I need to check your reading material."

"I'm very mature for my age, Mother. Ask my great niece here. She'll tell you."

Mac smiled. "It's true. I find her quite intelligent and well versed on many topics."

Mags said, "I'm worldly. Books take me places I may never see. I was just visiting India last week. I can be a traveler and never leave home."

"Books are safer, trust me."

"But you must have a purpose," said June. "What if it is me and Stan? Do you think we're a lost cause?"

"No. I think there's hope for you two. I watched the way his eyes softened when you touched his hand. You need to break down that wall he's got. Stan acts tough but I bet he's a scaredy-cat under all that exterior."

June giggled. "He might be. He's always puffing up, being such a braggart, but to be honest, I've never even seen him with a girl in a serious way."

"So, maybe he was telling the truth tonight when he said he was shy."

Mags said, "If he's shy, you've got to be bold, June. Read Joan of Arc before the morning and that will make you bold."

"I don't have time to read a book. It's getting late."

Mags yawned. "That never stops me."

Mac figured she would be asleep soon enough.

Violet said, "June, I think we need to get a place prepared for Mac to stay with us for the duration."

"Hopefully, it's just for the next few minutes, and I'll disappear like Chancellor did. Him showing up and moving out the way he did answered that question for me. I think I'll blink and be back to my time."

"Maybe so," answered June. "Until then, do you want your hair curled, too? We have extra rollers. Momma, you wouldn't mind, would you?"

"Not at all."

"It looks like I might miss my hair appointment at Sara's. I'd love it if you could."

Mackenzie felt an overwhelming sense of love from a family that was hers, but that she'd just met. They were the same. In so many ways. Mac loved that she was having this chance to meet the people behind the names of a family tree that sat drawn out with boxes and lines in a box in her closet box back home. Even though she felt a part of her was missing being away from her time, knowing that she was here, in the warmth of her home, with a whole new set of family that took her in unconditionally let her know that she came from the giving kind. It gave her a strange feeling of hope.

June's face spread into a wide grin. "When I curl my hair in these things, it stays bouncy for days."

Mags touched the crown of her head. "And it hurts right on top for days, too."

Mackenzie sat back and let the night happen. The talk of boys and telling them all about Jordan was safe enough. She wouldn't give them anything relevant to their time or life changing, only how Jordan changed hers in all the ways that mattered. There was a man of her dreams in a far away land, Mags reminded her. The fairytale could come true. She'd need to figure out her own happy ending.

Traveling Man

The voice died off. It wasn't Mrs. Hart or Aunt Shelby through the door. He knew that. He could hear their chatter, even though it was like a distant sound. The voice was something else unexplainable to be able to mark down in the book of his life with Mac.

Jordan exhaled and felt around him. He hoped that he'd notice some kind of rearrangement of sorts. Maybe see a portal open up or a secret door. He slid his hand around the walls. Smooth. It was the same type of carpet that extended from the hallway and pieced in the bottom of the closet. There was no opening that would give him a playground slide into an alternate reality.

His phone dinged. Service. If he had a signal, he wasn't in 1955. It was probably Jake wondering if he was coming home. He needed to stay close to Mac and Jolly so he was going to stick it out at her house overnight in case she reappeared. His parents were coming into the airport tomorrow. Their rehearsal and dinner were to begin at seven. How was he going to explain all of this, he wouldn't know? His parents would never let him live this down.

Ding.

He could try to ignore it. It dinged again. Triple texts meant it was his mother. She always wrote in short choppy messages. Ding. Another one.

Jordan pulled the phone from his pocket. What would he say? How could he tell them what was happening when he didn't even know himself? He texted her how he was ready to see everyone too and that he loved her. That would be enough until tomorrow. He hoped so anyway.

Jordan murmured, "You can let me out now."

He heard the voice of Aunt Shelby through the door. "It's not like we locked you in."

"Maybe you should. Maybe it's the key."

Mrs. Hart said, "It's just an old skeleton key. Have you been watching any fantasy movies lately, dear? There are no magic toy cabinets with special keys to twist the lock. There are no magic wardrobes here."

"Well, I'm sitting in this closet contemplating how this all could be. Humor me. Can you lock me in?"

Aunt Shelby said, "Can we get you on a recording to say we didn't lock you in, dear. Just in case we can't get you out. We don't need a murder charge this late in life."

Jordan said, "No one is getting a murder charge. Let's see if it's the key. I have to try."

He wondered if lights would flash or the closet would spin like the Rings of Fires & Flame ride at the state fairgrounds. Maybe he would lose consciousness and wake up in a dream. Is that what happened to Mac? Was she somewhere lost in time or only fast asleep?

"Here we go," said Aunt Shelby. "Steady now. Knock once if you stay and two if you go."

Mrs. Hart huffed. "I don't think it works that way, Shelby. And if he's gone, how's he going to knock."

Jordan hid a laugh because he was sure they would still be able to hear it. That Shelby was a piece of work.

He tried to get them refocused on the task at hand. "It's getting hot in here. Stuffy. Can you please turn it?"

"Let me do it."

"No, let me."

The voices rose and fell outside of the door and Jordan shook his head, hitting the sides of his knees with a tick tock motion of a pendulum in a clock.

He heard the scraping of metal against metal. The key was in place. Jordan held his breath. The turning of the key could bring Mac back.

Or not.

Nothing happened.

"Dear Lord, please take me to Mac. Please let me find her and bring her home safe. Amen."

No flashing lights. No disappearing arms and legs and vanishing into thin air. No movie dramatics.

It was only Jordan, sitting with a crooked hat, and a broken heart.

Answered Prayers

Violet was trying to keep June preoccupied and calm in the front seat by drawing her attention to the radio.

"Listen, June. *It's Only You.*"

Mac piped up from the backseat singing along, exaggerating her voice to try to match The Platters. "I love this song."

Violet asked, "You listen to our music."

"Of course. The 50s have the best music. I love it."

Violet said, "Okay, stop brooding, June. You're taking Mac on a tour of our town."

"I'm sorry. I'm worried about the falls."

"He'll be there," said Mac. "I feel it."

"Do you know it? Do we have a story?"

Violet interrupted, "Live in the moment, June. Have fun today. I'll be back around in a couple of hours to pick you girls up. Call me from the visitor's center if your plans change."

"We will, Mother. Thanks for the ride."

Violet asked, "Do you see Stan's car?"

June's voice was dejected, "No."

Mac put the optimism back in the air. "Not yet. Let's go for a walk, June. I love this place. I'm sure nothing much has changed. I'll show you where I'll be getting married and where the reception will be."

June smiled. "I can't wait to see. Come on."

Mackenzie walked with her grandmother down the hiking path that would take her to the bridge where Jordan and her were to be married. "Do you come down here in December? When the falls begin to freeze?"

"Yes, it's a gorgeous sight."

"So, now you know why I wanted a Christmas wedding. Other than that being my absolutely most favorite time of the year, God sure knew how to create a picture-perfect sight when he made the falls."

She made it to the bridge and was happy to see it was still there, exactly like it was in her time. Some things never needed changing. There was a bench that wasn't there in her time, and she grabbed June's hand and led her there.

"Do you think I'm here for me or for you?"

June asked, "What does that mean?"

"What if I'm here because I'm scared."

"Of what?" June laughed. "You can't be scared of anything."

"I'm keeping something from Jordan. Do you think that's why I'm back here? In this time? To show me that it doesn't matter where I go, if I'm with Jordan I'll be home. Like I had to miss him to understand that us being man and wife means if he has new opportunities, I need to support them, not wish for the complete opposite?"

June shook her head, and her curls did bounce in such a cute way that Mac couldn't help but spring one down and back in place. "I don't know what in the world you're talking about Mac."

Mackenzie told her all about her fears of leaving Crystal Falls. She didn't want to give up the relationships she'd built, leave her parents, or her school. She loved her home, and the thought of giving that all up to move into an apartment in the city made her heart hurt. She'd hid it from Jordan the minute he started to talk about it.

"How can I tell Jordan all of this without standing in his way of advancement?"

"As much as you've told us about Jordan, he seems like he would be so understanding. He would want to know, Mac. And here you were giving me the whole speech about being honest." ·

She leaned her head on June's shoulder. "I know. I'm sorry. I'm a mess, I guess. This might be all about me. When I get back, I'll find a way to say it all.

June said, "I know what you can do. You can write him a letter. That sounds like the best way these days to say how you feel when it gets really hard."

"Maybe I will. But first, I want to marry him. Then, we'll talk about all of that, and if Jordan still wants to go, if he gets a job offer, I'll follow him without standing in his way. I wish I could say to him to stop looking for jobs. I don't want to start a family in the city but stay in Crystal Falls."

"Are you already talking about a family, Mac?"

"Yes. We'd love to have a baby soon. Jordan and I both agree about that. If I can get up my courage to talk to him about not moving, then we will be on point."

"On point?"

"It means that we will be smooth sailing, like we see eye to eye on everything else. Just that one point of contention that he doesn't even know about. I can't believe I didn't tell him from the first conversation he had about applying. In his mind he thinks that if he gets a higher paying job, we'll be able to have a better family life. But family life doesn't mean tons of money, but more time. If we move into the city, I'm not sure we'll have that."

June leaned back on the bench and crossed her legs. "I believe in you, Mac. I know that you'll be able to talk to Jordan when the time is right, and you'll work things out. Thanks for telling me to write the letter, by the way. Even if Stan doesn't show, I needed to do it. Now, when I go back to State, I won't be carrying Stan in my heart. I can maybe meet a new guy."

That's when Mackenzie saw him coming. "Or maybe not."

"What is it? You don't think it's meant to be?"

"Oh, I think something is meant to be, and he's walking this way carrying roses."

"Roses?"

"Red ones. Not yellow ones for friendship, but red ones symbolizing love. Stan has a little romance in mind. I might need to let you guys have a moment. I can find my way back. I know these trails by heart. This is my favorite place to be in the world, regardless of the time."

She heard Stan call out, "Hey, June."

"Hey Stan."

Mac smiled as she made her way down the planked bridge and turned the bend to take a higher slope. She said, "Is this it, God? Because if it is, I'm ready to go back home. You can take me back now. I'm going to face what I need to with Jordan after the wedding. I know it will work itself out. Just take me home."

Searching for Answers

An intense feeling swelled up in Jordan's stomach as he pulled himself out of the closet. He sat on his knees, his hands resting on the carpet, wanting to dig in and scream but couldn't.

He didn't want to worry Mrs. Hart and Aunt Shelby any more than they were.

"I think that was for the best anyway," said Mrs. Hart. "What if you would have prayed your way out or back somehow, and you would've found yourself in another time. This time traveling is a dangerous business that must not be meant for us all."

"But it was meant for Mac? Do you know anything else about anyone in your family? Any other tall tales you might have dismissed as bedtime stories?"

Aunt Shelby said, "Did you see that box with all those strange symbols on it? The hat box? It almost looks like hieroglyphics etched on the sides. What do you remember about Grandma Violet's grandfather? Any stories?"

They made their way back to Mac's bedroom, and Jordan pulled out her laptop and decided he could do his own digging without having to depend only on the contents of the closet. Now was his time that he could research while they dug through boxes for any sign of Chancellor Mackenzie.

Mrs. Hart found a picture of a man wearing the very hat that was still positioned on Jordan's head. He was a handsome young man, with a bright smile and a mischievous gleam in his eye. Jordan noticed right away that he had some cockiness about him. Like he knew the secrets of the universe, and no one else did. If that can be sensed from an old black and white photograph, then that was the feeling from Chancellor.

"Have you ever registered for the ancestral sites, built any trees?"

Aunt Shelby said, "No. I wish we would have. My dad loved that genealogy stuff and even wrote a biography about his side of the family in anecdotal notes he would take from our family reunions. But our mom's side was more about Grandma Violet and our momma passing us stories. They were the storytellers, and I swear to you, I thought that's all this stuff was. Fairytales and fantastical spider web weaving of tales, until now."

Mrs. Hart put her hand over her mouth. "I got it. Wasn't he some kind of professor? History and such. I always remembered that part because when Mac was so fascinated with history at a young age, I knew that it had to come from him, and I'd tell her so. History runs in the family, dear. But what if..."

"Oh! He could be a traveler, too," said Shelby. "It sure hasn't been any of us, Janice. If so, I would've swish myself right down the black sands of Hawaii right about now, and we wouldn't be having this conversation. See ya."

"But the professor. Look him up, Jordan. The computer is finally up."

Jordan went right to work. He was a Duke University professor in the 1930s. The articles of him standing beside crates of artifacts being presented to the British Museum claimed he was a renowned researcher and field archeologist. He had articles in scientific journals, with a mile-long resume of accomplishments. The words expert, antiquities, world traveler added to his name.

"World traveler," said Mrs. Hart, "How about time traveler?"

"He is never seen without this hat. Jordan, you're wearing a mighty famous hat right now."

"With no telling what kind of germs," he snickered. "Let me sit it right here for now. It's not the hat. It's not magic."

They all heard a bell sound and turned toward the computer. A box appeared on the screen, with a green border, Celtic symbols on the corners, like a decorative card. Not a messenger box that Jordan was used to.

The words appeared across the screen. "Why are you so interested in Chancellor Mackenzie?"

Aunt Shelby squealed. "I'm telling you now, people. We're smack in the middle of a prank. An elaborate hoax. Some kind of movie in the making. Did you hear of any movie crews nearby? Did they rig up my house for some live paranormal movie?"

Jordan looked to Mrs. Hart. "You know I have to do this, right?"

"Yes, son. Go on. Let's see where this will lead."

"What do I say?"

"Always the truth. That's the only way to start."

He smiled, remembering a talk he'd had with Mac once about his family, and that's what her words of encouragement were to him. The truth. Even though he didn't quite know what that was. He would say what he knew.

"My fiancé, Mackenzie Hart is missing. We think she's gone."

Aunt Shelby said, "Take off gone and speak straight facts. Say time traveler. Get it out there."

There was no way for Jordan to bring it back. The box disappeared as soon as he finished the last word.

"What do we do now," said Shelby. "We might have missed our chance."

"We wait," said Jordan. "There will be a reply. I have a feeling we aren't talking to a generated computer message, but are having communication with Chancellor Mackenzie himself."

"But how can that be," gasped Mrs. Hart. "He's been dead for years."

Jordan raised his eyebrow. "That you know of, right? The unexplained yet again. I'm starting to believe anything is possible with your family. Mac chose me, for one. That was pretty much impossible. What were my chances of finding the love of my life? Mac's it. She loved me back. If that can happen, I can be talking to a guy that died..."

Aunt Shelby interrupted. "I have his death certificate in our box right here. April 2, 1940. Rusted razor blade. Infection to the face."

"Seriously? He died shaving? Could that happen?"

Jordan rubbed his face and felt his own stubble. Maybe he'd let it grow a little. He loved a beard in winter but was trying to keep it clean shaven for the wedding.

His wedding was in two days, with no Mac in sight.

The green box reappeared. "Missing, you say?"

Aunt Shelby bumped his arm. "Let me do it." She leaned over and slowly typed the words, "Time traveler," in all caps.

Mrs. Hart said, "I think the word is bold enough, Shelby."

"Well, we're going to get it all out there, aren't we? If this is the FBI, we haven't murdered anybody."

Jordan asked, "What is this reference to murder, Shelby? You keep bringing this up. You ladies are starting to worry me."

"Honey, it's the shows I'm watching. If we aren't getting pranked right now, we could be on some FBI case about to break wide open. But we aren't the criminals."

"I don't think there's been any crime," replied Jordan. "Just a missing person that happens to be hanging out with June."

"Agreed," said Mrs. Hart. "There's no reason to get all dramatic, Shelby. My nerves are torn up enough. No more talk about FBI or murder or anything kookie."

"Honey, this whole thing is kookie. Look, it's typing back."

"He," said Jordan. "I'm sure it's Chancellor."

It was a one-word response this time, but enough for them to know they piqued the interest of the mysterious messenger.

"Proof?"

Jordan took over the keyboard. There was no attachment clip for him to send the photos.

"Photos."

"That's all?"

"That's enough."

"Your location has been found. See you soon."

The box disappeared.

Aunt Shelby took Mrs. Hart by the hand and said, "Crank up the music, and let's dance." She swirled her around the papers and the boxes still scattered around the floor.

"This isn't the time to dance," scoffed Mrs. Hart. "We need to pray."

Aunt Shelby spun her around anyway. "Will he use the closet or the front door? Will he be young or old? Will he know us from this time or another? It's all so fabulous, if you ask me."

Before they could respond to Aunt Shelby's giddiness, the doorbell rang.

"Well, at least that answers one of my questions for the evening. Let's go my lady and dashing young fellow. Funny if you should wear the hat. Might be a nice touch."

Jordan grabbed the hat as she grabbed his hand and pulled him along. Jolly was already ahead of them, excited to meet the new visitor as much as them. Jordan figured Jolly was the one that probably held all the secrets of the universe. If only dogs could talk.

Mrs. Hart called out, "Who is it?"

"It's me."

"Well, that explains a lot."

"You just sent me a message."

Jordan said, "Why aren't we opening the door?"

All three of them stood rooted to the spot. Jordan looked at himself in the hall mirror and quickly put on the hat. Mrs. Hart was clinging onto Aunt Shelby as if she had already seen a ghost. In her hand, she held the picture of the young, Chancellor Mackenzie.

Aunt Shelby said, "Y'all are a bunch of bawk-bawk chickens." She swung open the door and smiled. "Welcome to the 21st century. Nice to meet you, grandpa of long ago."

The young man at the door laughed a bellowing sound that could only be described as cartoonish. Jordan leaned over and studied the picture in Mrs. Hart's hand. She was really shaking now, and he said, "This is exactly what we prayed for. Answers, remember? I think he might have them."

"I sure do, young man. And you have something that belongs to me. I've been looking for that."

In a sweeping fashion of feet spinning and arms extending, only to be mastered by the likes of Fred Astaire, the hat was no longer

on Jordan's head but flipped to the stylish, and ever so charming
man in front of them.

Mac found herself aimlessly walking through the trails, missing Jordan and Jolly, and everything about her time. It felt the same but different all at the same moment, and her heart felt as if it could break into a million pieces. She was giving June time to talk her feelings out with Stan, but she had to admit that being alone, even at the falls, made her feel more isolated than she'd ever felt.

Mac wiped the tears from her face. "God, I know you're here with me, even now. Can you please show me what I'm supposed to do?"

"Hey, girl. What'cha crying for?"

Two boys were walking, one was wearing a uniform as if he were in a boy's club and the other was carrying a whittled walking stick and a guidebook in his hand. Mac caught a glimpse of different types of trees, etched drawings of the bark and leaves that were to help them identify the species on their walk.

"I'm okay."

"You sure, lady? If you're lost, we can help you. Can we help you? We can get a badge for saving a life."

Mac smiled. They looked like they could be in her sixth-grade class. "Maybe I am a little lost." She didn't want to tell them it was more about her emotional state than her physical one. Mac would let them have their day of adventure.

The one boy with the field guide said, "Have no fear. We're here to serve you, ma'am. Follow us. We know the way of these lands."

"You do? Do you walk here a lot?"

He corrected her. "We don't walk. We hike. We take hiking trips, and we've camped out in the wilderness before."

"Twice," said the other boy.

"What's your names? I need to know them so when I get back to town, I can tell everyone about the boys who saved me from days of wandering in this vast forest."

The boy with the guidebook said, "I'm William Watson, but you can call me Bill. They all know me as Bill."

"And I'm Cal Potter. I'm in fourth grade."

She wasn't exaggerating that. "Wow, I would have taken you boys for at least sixth."

Bill said, "Golly! Really? And how long have you been out here? Days, you say? How have you survived? Do you have a survivalist guide?"

Mackenzie held her laughter but couldn't help but crack a smile. "Oh, I meant you saved me before it turned into days. I've heard your name before, Bill."

"Where from, I wonder? Maybe you read about my group in the paper. We did a big yard cleanup. My picture was right on the front page of the *Falls Times*. My mother had to frame it."

"I bet she was proud."

Mackenzie kept trying to remember why she would know the name Bill Watson. It's not like he was part of her family.

Cal said, "Maybe you know me, too?"

"Maybe. I know I'm really thankful I ran into you guys when I did. I was feeling pretty alone out here under the trees."

That wasn't far from the truth at all. She was actually right on target there. The boys were a great distraction for her. She hadn't flipped back yet. She was sure of that. Something was needing to be done, but she couldn't for the life of her figure out what was rooting her down to this spot.

Bill said, "While we walk, we can identify the trees and get two badges at once."

"That sounds like a good idea. I know a little about trees," said Mac, wanting to help out the boys while she could.

They talked trees and Mac taught them all about the different ways to tell from the bark to the leaves to the seeds they produced. The boys were impressed with her knowledge.

Cal said, "Are you sure you're lost, lady? You know a lot about this forest stuff."

"I read books."

Bill laughed. "You sound like Margaret. She always says that any time she gets the right answer. It's like she thinks she's the only one in the world that reads a book. Look at this. It's a book."

"It's a field guide."

"That's still a book, Cal. It counts as a book, and I'm reading it. I've been reading it."

"That's how I know your name."

"How?"

"Margaret. She mentioned you."

As soon as the words left Mackenzie's mouth, two large patches of red formed underneath his clear, blue eyes. "What did she say? Did she call me an idiot? I bet she thinks I am."

"I'm not so sure about that, Bill. I think that…"

Her voice caught, and she froze in her tracks. By the look on her face, the guys turned to follow her gaze. Bill turned back to them and held up the book. He waved it in front of them as if to silently let them know the answers were right in the palm of his hands.

Mackenzie prayed that the boys would know exactly what to do because she had no clue. Her heart pounded drum beats in her ears. As many times in her life that she'd taken a hike at the falls, she never had an encounter such as this.

A brown bear was making its way toward them, slowly sniffing its way along the brush, and Bill's hand on her shoulder let her know he was way calmer than she.

Bill turned to a section in a book as quietly as he could without making a sound. He showed them a picture of a boy laying face down with a pack on his back, still with wide legs stretched out on the ground. The three of them got down into the position and remained there for what seemed like an hour. Mac knew it was only minutes, but the time seemed to drag on. They could hear the sniffing and snorting of the bear, and finally when it lost interest, it made its way up the slope, the way they'd traveled from.

Bill peeked his head up and peered around. "The coast is clear. I think it's time we take a hike right out of here."

Cal said, "That was a close encounter if I have to say so myself."

Mac found her voice again. "Too close for comfort. I've never seen a bear up close before."

"I never want to see one again," said Cal. "That was enough for me. Look in the badge book. Do we get a badge for our quick thinking?"

"Maybe so," said Bill, checking off the list with the tip of his finger. "I think they need to give us every single badge for our bravery through it. And this lady didn't even cry."

Mac laughed. "Maybe I cried out all my tears before you guys found me. That was smart of you to know exactly what to do."

"Tell that to Margaret next time you see her. Tell her I read it in a book, and it saved our lives."

"I will be sure to tell her the whole story. I'm sure it'll be the talk of the dinner table this evening."

She felt so relieved when she saw Stan and June holding hands on the bench. "Guys, you won't believe what happened. We came face to face with a bear."

Stan said, "And I came face to face with an angry woman in love. I think we both made it out alive. I don't see any scratches."

"On you either. These boys saved my life."

She wasn't fibbing now. If they hadn't come along when they did, and she would've run into the bear alone she would've probably done the complete opposite of the moves they made to lie low until the bear passed. She might've screamed and ran for her life, provoking the bear even more.

Stan made a big deal out of it, and the boys beamed with pride. Mackenzie whispered to June about how Mag's crush was right there in front of them acting as hero, and he would be a perfect little gentleman for Mags one day. Mackenzie would never forget the way he blushed at the mention of Mags talking about him. Another little matchmaking attempt would've been successful until the bear happened to step into their view. That changed the subject quick.

Bill and Cal were adamant they met their father's in the parking lot and were excited to retell the story for the second time of how they saved the woman and fended off a bear attack. She was sure they might make it in the paper. She'd had her picture taken enough in 1955, so she'd relinquish the spotlight on this one. The boys made sure Mac corroborated their story, so that way their parents would believe them. It would've seemed like a far-fetched tale to Mac if she wasn't the one in the middle of the forest laying out flat on the ground.

Mr. Watson said, "What's your name, miss? In case they might want to feature this in the *Falls Times*?"

June said, "She's a celebrity around here. That's Mackenzie Hart. My best friend."

"Can I take a picture of you ladies?"

"As long as I get a copy of it later. I'd love it for my scrapbook."

The other dad pulled out his camera as well. "Can I have one with you and the boys?"

"Sure thing," Mac said. "Why not."

They posed for a few pictures and Mac watched them as they drove off. The boys were talking animatedly to their father's and knew this would be a story they'd share for a lifetime. Violet was turning into the parking lot, and Mac caught a glimpse of her car before June.

Stan had his arm around June's shoulder, and he was growling like a bear at her. He hadn't matured in the last two hours, and Mac couldn't help but do the June habit of rolling her eyes. But whatever it was that Stan was about, June got him. And she loved him the way he was. The same way Mac and Jordan fit together, making perfect sense.

"June, I think I'm going to head back with your mom. Maybe Stan could take you home later?"

June looked to Stan, waiting to see his next move. She ribbed him, and he finally spoke. "Oh, yeah. June, would you like to have dinner with me?"

June winked at Mac. "Sounds lovely. But you'll have to go ask my mother."

"Really?"

"Really? Well, if I have to ask her to take you to dinner, I might as well ask her can I go ahead and marry you already."

June's hand flew to her chest again. Mac was already picking up her grandmother's patterns. *Hold that heart, Grandma. It's about to race away.*

"Don't kid me, Stan."

"I'm not, June Darling. Right here, I'm asking you. Will you be my wife?"

"Just like that?"

"As a matter of fact, yes. Just like that."

"Well, I was wondering how long it would take you to ask me."

"Is that a yes? Your momma is waiting."

June put her arms around Stan's neck and said, "Yes, Stan the Man."

"No. It's Stan Your Man. I think it's time to change that up now that you're my girl."

"And forever that's what I'll be."

Mac stepped aside as June and Stan ran up to the car window. She could hear Violet scream out in the car and saw the fake swoon as if she were fainting in surprise. Violet probably saw it coming a mile away.

Why hadn't she flipped yet? What more could there be? She helped June connect with Stan. She helped the boys in the woods have an awesome memory. What else was there to do, and why was she feeling so stuck here in the past? With this last day coming to a close, she feared that her chances of marrying Jordan on time were growing slim. Would he still be waiting for her?

Puzzle Pieces

So much was a mystery in life. How God created the heavens and the earth, made the flowers bloom from a tiny seed, the size of a speck of sand in his hand, and setting the world in motion always fascinated Jordan. The birth of a child and knowing He knew the forming of the baby in the womb was a miracle as close as Jordan could imagine. Jordan knew deep down he was part of God's plan even if he didn't quite know how he fit into all of it.

Mac was always so sure. She was raised in church, with parents who read her Bible stories. She had a Sunday School teacher that she still visited on Saturday afternoons to check in on her even after all her years. Jordan didn't have those kinds of memories or connections with other people. Until Mac showed him it was possible, he wouldn't even have imagined life could be led in such a simple way.

He felt so wound up most of the time. Worried and stressed about how he could make Mac's life better. All of that would play with his mind while he was away from Mac. God, her, his family or lack of it, the town…All of it got him thinking. Now, he realized that he would spend a lifetime thinking about this new life with Mac, and with time travel in the same sentence, he had to relinquish the control over it because he had none. Trying to wrap his mind about the science behind time travel and infinity, Chancellor escaping death, and dimensions added to his realization that he knew so little about so many things.

Even with all the mysteries, there was a strange peace about him. That didn't scare him. Not knowing about the behind the scenes of life didn't bother him as he thought it would. It only made him more in awe of how God worked, even when he didn't understand it all. What did frighten him was that Mac might be scared somewhere, trapped, or worse...

For one man staring at them with answers made it even more intriguing. How did he get here? How did it happen to one person and not the other? Would he tell the truth or was this someone he couldn't trust?

Jordan watched as the man pilfered through all of their boxes, commenting about his very family, some he had an opportunity to meet along the way of his traveling life, and others he failed to do so.

"I've met Mackenzie once, long ago. It was her first traveling experience, and I could see the worry in her about not getting back. I had to show her firsthand how it works. Here one minute, gone the next. Maybe that eased her mind at least on how this life works. It might be time I make it back to 1955. We'll see if that's where I'm headed next. I've given my life over to this work, so I'm making no promises that it'll take me where you want me to go. It's not up to us in the end, after all. May I borrow this picture? I'll be sure to return it some way or the other."

He slid the picture of June and Mac in his inside coat pocket and patted it. "So, ask me away. I'm sure you have a long list of questions."

Mrs. Hart started round one. "How do you travel between decades?"

"Decades?" Chancellor leaned back and chuckled. "Dear, I can go through centuries, millennia, if I so choose to do so."

She pressed him. "But how? It isn't through the closet in the hallway because you used the front door."

"No. Traveling is not connected to a particular place."

"An object, then?" asked Jordan. "Like your hat, for instance?"

"My hat is a very sturdy hat. Nothing magical though, only my favorite hat. But objects that do hold great meaning could have the possibility to connect us to a particular time. If we are meant to be there, then the path will be made straight."

Aunt Shelby grabbed the framed picture she brought with her. "If I'm hearing you right, you say that if you're meant to be there, it happens. So, it's for a purpose? One that you might not even realize?"

"Oh, yes. Not to brag or appear to have a narcissistic personality, but I do have a quick wit about me, with an intellectual capacity well beyond my years. I figure out pretty quickly on most travels what God has tasked me to do. Others, well…let's just say, only God knows."

Mrs. Hart asked, "Do you see these people? We don't know them. We have no iota who in the world they are but they were all smiling on my living room mantle. How can they be there in that frame, belonging in my house, if I have no clue who they are?"

"Memories are tricky like that. When your Mac travels back, and the assignment has been fulfilled, all of the puzzle pieces will create an arrangement that fits nicely in your mind. You'll see the bigger picture, along with the minor color variations, and how all of it fits into place."

Jordan said, "I feel like we've got a few missing puzzle pieces too many."

"My degrees are in history not philosophy or physics. The only mechanics I know is how to change the oil in my Chevy truck, nothing close to quantum mechanics. Don't ask me the tough stuff, kid. Only surface. Let's swim the top of the pool, not dive below."

Mrs. Hart said, "Why did it happen to Mac?"

"First, I love her name. Must have come from me, I suppose."

"My mother June passed along a wild tale of a story to me and always begged me to name my daughter Mackenzie and call her Mac. I didn't know it was so that she would be named after you. That's a surprise to me. I thought it was because she met Mac in the past and connected the puzzle pieces together."

Jordan cut in, "But why Mac? Why can she travel, and I can't?"

He crossed his arm and folded his legs, leaning back against the bed frame. "So, you tried?"

Aunt Shelby said, "He was praying in the closet wearing your hat."

"Well, at least you got the prayer part right. I'm not sure why the good Lord above chose me to do His mission possibles, but He did."

Mrs. Hart smiled. "Because all things are possible with God. Nothing is impossible. See, Jordan. It's a Biblical thing, not scientific at all."

"So, can I go back?"

"No, that's impossible."

"But you just said…"

"It's not for me to decide if I can take you back with me. It must be part of God's plan. There's a reason Mac is back. So, I say let her be. Eventually, after days, or months, or even a year, she'll find her way back to you. When the time is right, she'll return."

"But, we're to be married in two days."

"Married, you say? Why that does put us in a pickle."

Aunt Shelby said, "I say that, too. We need a pretty big jar for all the pickles we've been having lately."

"So, let us not worry any longer."

Jordan smirked. "You don't know my parents. They won't understand why Mac isn't at the rehearsal dinner tomorrow."

Chancellor's voice grew serious. "Will you wait for Mac?"

"No doubt."

"Then, wait for Mac."

Mrs. Hart said, "What if she can't come back?"

He laughed. "God gives us a temporary assignment with our travels. It's not like we are in it to win it for the long haul. He sends us on a mission, not a permanent stay."

Aunt Shelby interrupted. "Mission possibles. I like the sound of that. Is it like MP, abbreviated, and do you have an FBI unit? Like an investigative team? Mission control centers or a guide?"

Chancellor laughed. "Television really does expand one's imagination."

Mrs. Hart said, "Or makes one dull."

"It's just me, hopping from here to there wherever the Holy Spirit leads. I follow. I really don't have a choice, now that I think about it. I'm here one minute, and maybe gone the next. That's why the traveling man is never able to settle down for long. It takes a mighty patient love to withstand the traveling ways."

"True love can withstand anything," Mrs. Hart's voice softened as she turned to Jordan. "Don't be discouraged, dear."

"Oh, it better be true or you'll be like Lucille. She decided it wasn't right for the two of us on account of her suspicious conspiracies and such. She thought I was hopping between women when I was collecting antiquities to showcase for the museum. Everyone wants proof these days. It's my job to give it to them."

"Proof of what?"

"God. Everyone needs a picture. A stone carving. A mosaic floor. A piece of pottery. An underground church. I discover them when God reveals the time and location. All by the workings of a power not my own but for His glory."

Jordan asked, "Mac majored in history like you. She's a teacher, not a professor. She has a faith that I'm in awe about, and wish I had a fraction of it. Do you think she's also meant to follow in your footsteps? Is that what Mac's called to do?"

"Now, that's between her and God to figure out her calling. I don't have the insider news flash about Mac. She'll come to discover it in her own time. Right now, I'm sure she's doing fine. Our people are a lively, strong stock. You don't worry about Mac's purpose. Wait. You pray about your own."

"My job is to stand by Mac."

"Then, if that's what you're called to do, it will be a hefty commitment you'll be making. Man and wife. One second saying vows…the next she might be in the rain forests of Africa."

Jordan asked, "And if that happens, what am I supposed to do?"

"You wait."

"And what do I tell people?"

"We always worry about trivial things, like what the neighbors will say."

Jordan laughed. "You don't know my mother. She'll ask me a thousand questions."

"She had an emergency with work and was called away on important business. Facts. Tell them facts. There's a charm to the simple truth. The Lord will take care of all." Chancellor pulled out a business card. "I even know what you're going to say next. Show them this business card if they need proof. Always proof."

Jordan said, "Well, you asked for proof. We had the pictures. Remember?"

"I guess it comes with the territory. I'm a product of my own interrogation."

Aunt Shelby inspected the card. "I knew it. See, you do have an abbreviation. MIA – Mackenzie International Antiquities – Past, Present, and Future. Preservation Specialists."

"Say she's one of us. She is, after all, my great granddaughter, you say?"

"A long line of greats. Think of great, great, great granddaughter."

"Now, that's a lot of greats."

"She is great."

Chancellor said, "Okay, now you're starting to sound like a cereal commercial. Television reference, again?"

Jordan said, "How can you appear so young? Do you not age?"

"Oh, I age. In fact, I die some time or another, but it hasn't happened yet, as you can see by my cherry disposition and light mood."

Aunt Shelby frowned. "For a traveler you don't seem too concerned. I'd be a worried somebody if I were flip flopping around on the face of a clock like some fish on a pier."

"Why be anything but willing to do the Lord's work? I'm not concerned one lick. I figure it's better to live my life with the tendency to accept what comes, meet the people I'm supposed to meet and hope it does some good."

Mrs. Hart said, "And does it?"

"Sometimes I believe it does. Any more questions before I travel on."

"Will you go to Mac?"

"I'm here with you because it was meant to be. You were praying for answers and the Lord heard. He takes special care of those who love Him and call upon His name."

Aunt Shelby popped the brim of his hat. "And the Lord sure does answer in strange ways."

Mrs. Hart said, "Hey, who are we to question the ways of God?"

Jordan hung his head. "You mean to say there are no other questions you'll answer? You'll only tell me to wait?"

"Wait. Go about your life. Take care of your business. Prepare the place for Mac as if you know she's returning. Be ready. She'll arrive when the time is right."

"But how do you know?"

"Because God is always right about these things. Have no fear, Jordan. The Lord is with you and with Mac, wherever she may go."

When Jordan lifted his head, Chancellor Mackenzie was gone.

That fast.

And that explained what happened to Mac.

No closets. No magic.

She was here, and then she was gone.

Just like Chancellor.

Mrs. Hart said, "There's no reason to fear, Jordan. We have to be at peace about whatever this is."

Aunt Shelby clapped. "*Peace like a River.* I love that song. Let's put on some music, continue to dance, and make this night a happy one. Mac's on a mission. A mission possible, with a power that can't be seen or reckoned with."

Jordan hit the song on his playlist. "And tomorrow?"

Mrs. Hart said, "Let tomorrow fend for itself. We have enough to deal with today."

"But tomorrow we face my family without Mac."

"She may come back. Just like that. A snap, crackle, and a pop."

Aunt Shelby said, "Forget the dancing. All this talk of cereal makes me hungry. Let's go get some food."

"Sounds like a plan," said Mrs. Hart. "Snack time."

Jordan stayed behind and picked up the picture of him and Mac beside her bed. It was at the falls where they first met. Where he proposed. She demanded they snap a picture as soon as the ring slid on her finger, saying she needed proof on the days when things might get tough. They'd never had a single tough day. It was all so easy with Mac. Everything made sense with her. Nothing made sense without her. Wonder if she knew the tough day would be the day without her in it?

None of this made sense but knowing that Mac was in the hands of God made him feel a little better about the whole traveling deal.

"God, I hope you have me in your hands, too."

Mrs. Hart came back in, overhearing his prayer. "It's a sure thing he does."

"Comforting, isn't it."

"Enough to make you stay sane in a crazy world."

"And a world with so much hurt, Mac could be a busy traveler indeed," spoke Aunt Shelby from the door. "Come on, sis. Time we got a move on. I think Jordan is the waiting kind."

Mrs. Hart asked, "You aren't going anywhere, are you?"

"Not a chance. Jolly and I will hold it down until Mac returns. When my family comes in tomorrow…"

Mrs. Hart said, "Remember what I said. Tomorrow is another day, and if it comes, I'm sure it will take care of itself."

Aunt Shelby grabbed Jordan by the face and kissed him on the forehead. "And if it doesn't, then I'll handle it. I've already got a plan on how to deal with your family if Mac hasn't arrived in time for the rehearsal. I'll be the stand in."

Mrs. Hart said, "That would be an interesting rehearsal for sure. Start praying, Jordan."

"I haven't stopped," he said, as he led them to the door. "Maybe it won't come to that. She'll be in my arms tomorrow night. That's the plan. Let's go with that."

"Don't forget my offer. I can make up some pretty tall tales myself. Got that honest from my momma. So, now I've realized they're all true. I bet I can stir up some pretty good lines to get the whole of Crystal Falls believing it. I'll show you."

Jordan said his last goodbyes and stood to face the emptiness of Mac's house. It wouldn't be Mac's home for long. They'd be moving soon for his new job in the city. He knew how much Mac loved living in this quaint little cottage style house. Everything about it screamed Mac. Except he wanted to scream out to her, to call out that he was waiting, but he was sure she wouldn't hear him.

"I'll write her another letter, Jolly. That's all I know I can do as I wait. I guess I might be writing a lot of these in my future after what Chancellor told us. You'll be my sidekick while we wait?"

Jolly sniffed as in reply.

"I thought so. You're the best. I bet your momma is missing you." Jordan patted Jolly on the head and thought to himself, *I hope she's missing me, too.* "She won't forget about us," he said to Jolly. He prayed that would be the case. Who knew about these kinds of things? It's not like Chancellor left him a manual. He could only pray their love could outlast the hands of time. He knew his would make it, and was counting on Mac to feel the same.

Maybe This 

Mac slid into the front seat and turned to look at Violet, hardly able to contain her excitement. "Well, that went better than expected."

Violet laughed. "You must've really worked your magic, Mac. Whatever it is that you did, it was successful. June is to the moon right now."

"All I did was nudge her to write the letter. That was the both of them working that out. I'm glad I could witness it. This whole thing is pretty magical if you ask me."

"So, you're still here, dear."

"I guess so. Wonder if that means I've got more to do?"

Mack leaned back into the leather seat of the powder blue Pontiac and settled in on the music. Violet was singing along to *That's All Right* by Elvis.

"If so, do you think you're going to stick around with us awhile, Mac? We'll make room for you. June is about to go off to school soon."

"I think I already planted an idea in June's head. She might be able to do her student teaching here at Crystal Falls for her senior year. She might be around doing her field work to be closer to Stan."

"Do you think he was serious about that marriage business back there in the parking lot, or do you think he was playing with her emotions?"

"Oh, he meant it," Mac said. "They get married in less than a month. I figured it was coming quick."

"A month! A wedding in a month? Are you serious, dear?"

"I've seen the marriage certificate to prove it."

"Well, that beats all I've ever heard. Do you know any of the details, so I don't panic?"

"None whatsoever. Other than the date. I've got that one down. It's coming. Let it happen."

"Maybe you're to stay here with us until the wedding is over? Maybe to help me stay grounded in what I could only imagine as being chaos. This whole trip could be to assist me as a fabulous wedding planner."

On the ride back home, all Mac could do was wonder what was this all for? If Chancellor could appear and tell her exactly what she was supposed to do or what was next for her, that would have been lovely. Instead, she sulked up the steps and into the house, trying to shake a feeling of sadness overwhelming her spirit as she made it to the den. Margaret was pacing the floor.

"Finally. I'm so glad you're back. Guess what! Guess what!"

Mackenzie wondered how the news of June and Stan's wedding traveled that fast without cell phones.

Violet asked, "What's got you screaming in the house? Where's your father? Wait until he gets hold of our news."

"Look at this."

Mags was holding a letter in her hands. She wondered if it was from Jordan. "Did you write to Jordan and he write you back?"

"No, silly. I can't write to the future, but I can write to my pen pal, Connie. She's been sick, Momma. And they're bringing her to the hospital close to here. The one in Silver Springs. They have a children's wing. Can I go see her? Please, Momma. Read her letter. Please."

Violet said, "I don't know, Mags. We'll have to see when all this could be and get plans together. We've now got your sister's wedding to plan."

Bruce barked, "Wedding? Did I hear you say wedding? Who's getting married in this house?"

"Stan asked for our permission to marry June, and of course I gave it to him. I was sure you wouldn't object."

"Why would I? I go along with whatever you ladies want."

Violet winked at Mac. "See, he's a good one. A keeper."

Mags sat cross legged on the couch. "Heavens to Betsy. Tell me the scoop. The whole shebang."

"Do you want the proposal, meeting Bill Watson, or the bear attack?"

Mags said, "Start with the middle and work your way to the outsides?"

"The middle?"

"Bill Watson was in the middle of your sentence. Start there."

Mac retold the story of Bill and Cal, and gave her all of the details, down to every word. Mags would say, "I don't think he's an idiot," to the next couple of interruptions, asking the question, "Why would he think I think he's an idiot?" Mac finally got the whole story out about the day.

"And here I was with this cold and couldn't go out. Momma, look what I missed with you making me stay cooped up in here all day."

"It was for your own good. What if you'd come face to face with that bear, and it would have smelled your sweet scent, thinking you were a bowl of scrumptious honey. I couldn't bear the thought."

"That's a good one, Momma. If I were keeping a point tally, you'd get one for that." Mags added, "I think I'd be more scared to come face to face with Bill Watson than a bear."

"He was a hero," answered Mac. "And don't forget I told you about those red marks across his cheeks. It wasn't from the heat, Mags. He was a blushing little boy over you."

Mags mirrored the same rosy complexion. "So, back to the wedding. If her hospital visit isn't around June's wedding, do you think I would have a chance to visit Connie? There's a number to call. Will you call it, Momma? Please?"

"Let me go ahead, or I'm sure I won't hear the end of it."

Mags hugged her mother with a fierce devotion. "Thanks, Momma. We've been writing for three years now. It would be great to see Connie in real life. I think I want to give her my doll, Mary. She'd probably love it. I'll go clean her up a bit."

Mags ran up the stairs to her room, and Mac knew she would be arranging dolls and making important decisions. Violet held the letter in her trembling hand.

"What's wrong?"

Violet sat down on the edge of the chair close to the phone on the side table. "I've spoken with Connie's mom already. I didn't have the heart to tell Mags. This letter is arriving a little late."

"Oh, poor Mags."

Violet started to cry as she read over the letter. "Poor Connie. She was diagnosed with polio earlier this year, and it's progressing. So many taken by this crippling disease. It breaks my heart beyond having the words for it to think of what this family is going through. She's Mags age, you know."

What harm could it be to tell Violet what was coming? It's not like it would change her course. Her heart was breaking, and she couldn't stand the thought of the same thing happening to Mags. "I'm vaccinated for polio. The vaccine works and will help to almost eradicate the disease. It might not help Connie, but the invention helps so many others and prevents the spread."

Mags walked in holding her doll, her eyes light with expectancy. "This is the one. She'll love it. Her name is Mary."

Violet straightened her shoulders and smiled. "She's very lovely. Isn't that one of your favorites, dear?"

"That's why I want Connie to have it. It's a collector's, too. See, I kept the tag on it to prove it. It's something I think she'll treasure and keep forever."

Violet looked up to Mackenzie, almost pleading with her to do something with her eyes. Mac said, "I'm sure she'd love it, Mags. Maybe I can take it to her. I can pass it along for you."

"Why? I want to give it to her."

Violet said, "I don't think that's a good idea, dear. Mac is here on a mission remember. It could be to give the doll to Connie. We thought it was about June, but it could very well be to bring you and Connie comfort right now. Think of Mac as a magical assistant, and she can go to the hospital in Silver Springs. We can set up the arrangements now. I was just about to call."

Mags sighed. "But Momma. I want to meet Connie face to face. She's my best friend."

"I know, dear. But you've been a little under the weather yourself, and it wouldn't be smart exposing Connie with all those germs you might still be carrying around in that nose of yours."

She twitched her lip and blinked heavily. Mac knew she was holding back tears. "If you say so, Mother." She put the doll down on the sofa and arranged her dress. "Mac, tell her I'll be praying for her. I'll write her a new letter that you can take with you."

"Sounds good, sweetie. I'll pass along whatever it is you'd like for me to carry."

"Carry my love to her, too."

"I will definitely do that."

Mac watched her walk away and turned to see Violet no longer able to hold back tears. "I have such a precious child."

"That you do. I completely agree with you on that."

"The Lord blessed me with June and Mags. We lost a couple of little ones to be with the Lord early. I believe they were both boys gone on to Heaven too soon. I dreamed of them each time they passed, playing in a field together of golden wheat." She stared up to the ceiling as if to catch a glimpse of them in Heaven. "I'm thankful for my two girls, and pray the Lord continues to bless their little hearts and give them a long life filled with happiness."

Mac didn't have it in her to tell her about what she remembered about Mags losing her life at a young age to sickness. Polio struck the very house that she was standing in. Those were the secrets that wouldn't be shared. She could pray that the course of Mags life would change. There was always hope. While there was breath there was hope. So, that's what she would hold on to. The hope that she'd get to see Jordan soon, before her wedding, and that all would work itself out for good in the end.

Stand with Me

The waiting wouldn't be easy, but Jordan knew no matter what he faced with Mac, as long as they had each other, the rest would work itself out. Her traveling days may just be beginning, but so was their life together.

Jordan took Chancellor's advice and went about his day, trying his best to push any doubts he might have had the day before about Mac out of his mind. He picked up his parents and older brother, Mark, from the airport. He told them that Mac was tying up last minute loose ends.

His mother rented out B&B's, a bed and breakfast that hosted large crowds. It was a picturesque lodge sitting right at a lookout point of the mountains he'd grown to love. More of his family would be arriving soon enough and the Aunties and long-distance cousins would keep his parents wrapped up without even worrying about Mac's lack of presence.

Jake was waiting for them to pick up the suits. Jake met his father, Leonard McLaughlin before, and Mark was always between his parents, one week at a time. Due to his severe Autism, he needed the constant care that his parents lovingly provided. At least they got that right in his life. If Jordan had to consider all things, he'd want his brother taken care of above all things. He understood the attention had to go to Mark. His whole life had been that way. Jordan had to learn early on that he had to take care of himself, because he was the one that could. He was okay with that.

Jordan's dad grasped his son's hand. "I know it's probably too late to tell you this, but single life is way better than tying the knot,

Jordan. You get to live it up. You're young, handsome, a rising businessman. Your mom told me about your new job."

"Let's keep that to ourselves, Dad. Mac doesn't know yet."

"Yeah, look at this town. It's a dead-end street, Jordan. There's nothing here."

Jake shook Mr. McLaughlin's hand. "I have to disagree with you, sir. I've grown to actually love this little town. I'm planning on sticking around and finishing up a master's degree here."

"Some girl got you here, too?"

"No, sir. I've decided it's good for me to stay here. Jordan is the antsy one, always wanting the next big thing."

"He got that honest. That's why I don't think you need to settle down just yet. Mackenzie is a beautiful girl, don't get me wrong. But...there are so many, Jordan. Why stick with one?'

Jordan couldn't believe he was actually having this conversation in the middle of Hegarty's, the men's suit shop downtown, on the day before his wedding. He was mortified. His dad wasn't the one to talk in a low voice, either. The louder his father got the more agitated Mark would become, and Jordan knew he had to get the conversation to a controlled level.

"Dad, I love Mac. No more, okay. I really don't need this right now."

"That's what I'm saying. Your mother spent all that money on that fancy mountain house, and she's always complained about not having any time for vacations. She's probably here just to party."

"Dad."

"Well, I'm speaking truth, son. You need to know what you're getting into with Mac. Women can lead you the wrong way in a hot minute."

Jordan felt humiliated. "And I'm sure you could do the same for women."

"Maybe so."

Jake was preoccupying Mark with the different color ties. He liked the patterns of the silk. When Mark turned around holding up two ties, Jordan smiled.

Jake said, "I think he wants to wear both."

Jordan grinned. "Which one, buddy?"

Mark stuck out his arms and waved the ties in front of him. "You want me to pick? I think Mac will like the red or the green. Both are Christmas colors, and she'll love them. Pick one for me and one for you."

Mark put both around Jordan's neck and turned him to the mirror.

His dad sneered. "See, even Mark knows you need more than one thing at a time to keep you going. That goes with ties and with women."

"Dad, can we please lower it down. I'm marrying Mac tomorrow. Please accept that and let's not talk about it anymore."

Mark said, "Both."

"I'll get both, buddy. I'll get both. I'll let you wear one, though."

Jordan looked to Jake, and he could read the embarrassment on his face. He knew it wasn't because of Mark. It was his father. His parents had a way of always bringing him down. If Mac were here, she'd find a way to help him turn it around. She had that way about her, and her optimism and gentleness helped him see the world in a new way.

Now, with Mac gone...

No, he wouldn't start that in the middle of the store. He was already feeling like he might lose it any second. So, he focused on straightening Mark's tie and then laughed when Mark jerked it from being tight. He didn't like them tight either. Maybe a bowtie for Mark would do. *Focus on what is right in front of you,* he thought.

Jake whispered, "Your dad is kind of a jerk. I'm glad you aren't, or I wouldn't be here right now."

"Yeah, he's a real piece of work. Help me with Mark, and let's take care of what we have to do. If we ignore my Dad, he'll eventually realize his audience has left the building and he'll simmer down."

"Until he finds his next audience?"

"Exactly. That's why it's best to keep him moving."

They finished up as quickly as they could in Hegarty's and tried to make the best of it for Mark's sake. Jordan was having a difficult time maintaining eye contact with his dad. He knew the negative remarks would continue if he let it. Sad to say his mother was not much different. The whole misery loves company concept always worked for them. Too bad they couldn't continue it together because now they could multiply and spread their negative energy.

When they finished paying for their suits, Jake said, "Mr. McLaughlin, how about you, me and Mark go down and grab a bite to eat. I know Jordan has a few things he needs to take care of before the rehearsal dinner tonight."

"But I've come all this way early to spend time with my boy."

"I'll catch up with you guys later. I promise. I do have to go check on some things at the falls before tonight."

"Alright then. Maybe you'll think about what I said. There's still time to back out. Up to saying I do. You've got your freedom. Even after that, you can sign another paper all the same and end it, too. It's only paper, son. It's a bunch of papers, either way you go."

Jake squeezed his shoulder. "Go on, Jordan. Maybe go for a hike, too. Clear your head a little. I've got this."

Jordan whispered, "I owe you."

"Plenty."

Jordan gave Mark a bear hug. One day he always prayed that Mark's arms would come around him and hug him in return. He knew Mark really wasn't one for showing affection. He would hug him anyway and never let it stop him. When they were kids, Mark would push him away. The more he stuck with hugging him, the more he eventually caved and let him do it. Never returning, but not pushing away either. That let Jordan know that his brother did love him. Or at least didn't mind.

"I'll see you in a little bit, buddy."

"Bye."

"Bye."

Jordan shook his dad's hand even though it was the last thing he wanted to do. It was still right. He shouldn't have expected any encounter any other way with his father. The reunion with his mother would probably run along the same path.

Jordan said as they started to part ways, "Are you okay?"

"Yeah," he replied, but knew that he wasn't. He should have eloped with Mac. As soon as Mrs. Hart found out about their engagement, she insisted on making family calls, announcements, and all the wedding planning began. He would have to include his family. Maybe if he'd been honest with Mrs. Hart about his family, she would've understood him sweeping Mac away the next weekend and they'd been married for months by now.

Two shops down, he found himself looking in the window of Mrs. Marjorie's dress shop. He caught a glimpse of Mrs. Hart in the store and knew it was meant to be that he walked in the opposite direction.

The bell jingled, and Mrs. Marjorie peeked her head around to sound out her welcome to customers. "Well, if it isn't the groom himself. I thought you were Mac. I've been waiting on her for the past half hour."

Mrs. Hart came up to him and put her arm through his. "What a nice surprise, Jordan. Just in time to help me pick out the dresses."

Mrs. Marjorie shouted, "But we need Mac for that. Where is Mac, anyway? She's usually joined at the hip with you, Janice. Time is of the essence."

Mrs. Hart said, "You have no idea, Marjorie. Let us do the shopping. You can go on back to tidying up or doing whatever you were up to before the bell jingle. Jordan and I will take care of the dresses. You take care of the alterations."

Jordan asked, "And how am I supposed to take care of Mac's dress?"

"It seems like you're here to pick out Mac's dress, dear."

"Her dress? She told me she found the perfect one months ago."

Mrs. Marjorie came back from around the corner. "Now, I would have you to know that it really was an accident. Janice, tell him so. Y'all don't start to tweety bird this mess out. I feel horrible enough already."

Mrs. Hart told Jordan the long story short. He frowned. "And Mac isn't here to pick out her own dress. So, what you're saying is when she gets back, she'll have no dress. That would be a little hard to explain to everyone if she isn't walking down an aisle in a wedding dress and the rest of us are fitted to the finest."

"Did you get your suit?"

"Just left it with Jake. I'm all set."

"Then, let's set this next part right. Let's go on about what we must take care of and prepare the way."

Jordan asked, "While we wait?"

Mrs. Hart tried to fix her face to wear a smile, but Jordan could sense her tension. She gritted her teeth and said, "While we wait."

He didn't know the first thing about picking out a wedding dress, but he did know his Mac. She loved anything vintage. *Shop Around the Corner* was her favorite movie, and now here he was in a shop down the main street of Crystal Falls right before Christmas shopping for her. He would find something perfect for her if it took him all day.

Mrs. Marjorie set up her cider in the corner with butter cookies from blue tins for customers today. It was the last-minute shopping day called, "Downtown in a Hurry," event that happened each year.

Mrs. Hart said, "It would have to be the busiest shopping day when we're having to do this, wouldn't you know it."

Busy meant there would be more eyes catching what Jordan and Mrs. Hart were up to. He prayed no one would notice them but knew better than that. His boss was even in the store picking out a dress for a banking event in the city she was invited to go to for their quarterly review meeting.

"I wasn't expecting to see you here today, Jordan. You should be two doors down at Hagerty's."

"I've already been. I'm just..."

Mrs. Hart interrupted, "He's helping me pick out my dress for the wedding. I've been so busy with all of the plans that I left out the part that I needed my own dress as mother of the bride. Jordan was kind enough to assist me."

"Jordan, you're one of a kind. After the reports I've spent the past two weeks combing over, I must say we need to talk at the new year. I think a raise and new position for you are in order."

Jordan hadn't told Mrs. Dunham that he wasn't planning on having any meetings with her but one, the day he placed the letter of resignation in her hand. She reached out her hand to shake on it as if it were already a done deal.

He shook her hand and her smile widened. Instead of saying they'd set an appointment time, her next words shocked Jordan. "Good thing I ran into you today. I like being able to give Christmas presents early. It's settled then. Let's go ahead before the new year and call you Assistant Manager."

She walked away and Jordan stood there stunned. Mrs. Hart squeezed his arm. "Lookie here, my new son got him a brand-new job title with a raise to go with it. Keep going, Jordan, and one day you'll be running the bank."

Jordan didn't know what to do with her praise. He was already making comfortable money in Crystal Falls, and now, with the possibility of a raise, he could really work that out and set him and Mac up right, especially with the cost of living and minimal bills. Maybe Jake was right. This town might have more to offer him than he ever dreamed possible. He respected the people he worked with and had formed solid collaborations with employees and the community. Mac's parents were so good to them. They'd raise a family where family mattered, not alone in the city.

Mrs. Hart asked, "Jordan, what's got you so stone silent. You look like you're making a pro/con sheet in your head. The one that means you're trying to make a big life decision."

He didn't' want to tell Mrs. Hart before Mac, but he felt led to do it on the spot. "I was offered a good job in Charlotte to start in January. Mac doesn't know. I had reservations at Mariana's to celebrate and tell her the news, but she didn't show. Remember."

"Oh," was all she said, and she turned back to the racks.

"I need to talk to Mac about this. She'll know what to do."

Mrs. Hart laughed. "Mac is a little biased you know. She'll chose this town. She loves Crystal Falls, Jordan. There's something about this place that's magical."

"Apparently."

"I don't know what it is about it, but it seems to call out to your soul. The simple runnings of the place. The kindness from everyone. It feels real here. Not some plastered on fake you can sometimes get from a place. It feels right."

"You sound like Jake. He's decided to stay around and get his master's."

"Lookie here. You've got Mac loving this place. Jake planting himself for another couple of years. There's this new job opportunity for you at the bank, and Mac adores her job. You already have the house. So much right here."

Jordan noticed she left her and Mr. Hart out. "And we would be close to you."

She beamed and Jordan knew it made her happy to be acknowledged. "That, too. Maybe with all of this new transition going on with Mac's side job, it might be a good idea to consider Crystal Falls. At least until we can figure this whole thing out. You'd have our support and be surrounded by family and friends."

"That's a good point. I think you're right. We don't even have to worry Mac about Charlotte talk. I'll send them an email and decline the offer." He knew there was no better time than the present, and he unlocked his phone in the middle of the aisle and began to craft the letter.

"Tell them a better one popped up. City jobs will always be there. There's so much we can do in this small town to help revitalize it and bring it back to its hay day."

"Like the day Mac might be walking in right now?"

"That very day. She might come back bursting with all kinds of ideas."

"We'll never stop her then."

"This talking is stopping us from picking out Mac's dress."

"Let's try to look a little less conspicuous."

Mrs. Hart stifled a laugh. "Honey, if you only knew how we looked over here. All mysterious over white dresses. Let's act like we're on a mission possible and get this done."

It didn't take Jordan long to find a long, flowing gown. Mrs. Hart held it up for inspection. They called out the features they felt Mac would love about it. The lace. The simple cut. The elegant layers in the front. Mrs. Hart checked the size.

"It's still going to need alterations. At least Mrs. Marjorie didn't spill wine on her logbook."

"Funny, dear. I heard that. And it was Scooter that did the spilling."

Jordan passed her the dress. "Do you think you could have it ready by the morning?"

Mrs. Marjorie said, "Come back tonight after your rehearsal dinner. It'll be fixed up, along with whatever Janice wants as a packaged deal."

"I know it's my turn. This time, Jordan, I'm sending you on your way before we get too many questions asked."

"Please do. The thought of Jordan already seeing Mac's dress worries me enough," said Mrs. Marjorie. "If people found out why…"

"I'm out, Mrs. Marjorie. Don't worry. Your secret is safe with me."

"Where is Mac, anyway?"

Mrs. Hart said, "Mac's on a mission, but she'll be back soon."

That was the end of that. Mrs. Marjorie was satisfied with the answer and went about her way.

Mrs. Hart said, "With Marjorie I was expecting the third degree. Maybe that's the magic answer. We can use that one line and it could be enough. Like angels themselves have laced the words with a secret coded message responding right to the spirit. Marjorie walked away smiling. That has to be a holy intervention."

"Let's hope it works on my mother."

He heard her voice from behind him. "What are you hoping works on me?"

Jordan turned to face his mother and his two Aunts from Washington. They were always together, the three sisters. If this was some secret Jedi message he could use on them, then it was better to try it out now while the magic might still be in the air.

"Mac's on a mission, but she'll be back soon."

"Good, dear. We're on a mission, too. We're here to find Mia an appropriate dress. Seems like she forgot we were to be out in the freezing temperatures. Sleeveless, really?"

They started to fight over the dress Mia brought with her, and Jordan knew it was his time to escape. Mrs. Hart chimed in on their discussion and started to lead them to the winter line. Aunt Mia was already holding up a fur collared red and black cocktail dress. Even though he didn't know much about his mother, the one thing he did know, she loved to shop and spend money.

She was a commentator at a local Washington station and prided herself on always looking the way she did on camera. Even at home, Jordan never remembered a time when he saw her in a relaxed state. She played the part, and it fit her well.

Her formalities were such a stark contrast to Mac's down to earth demeanor. Thinking of all the ways they were so different, how unlike he was to his own family didn't make him feel isolated because he knew how he fit with the Hart family. He had a place where he could be himself. He made his way down to the end of the main street to find his car, but then thought to circle back to the diner to check on Jake and Mark.

He called Jake to see if they were still there. Jake told him they were having a great time, and to go on about his day. They'd see him later at the rehearsal dinner.

Jordan hoped they'd see Mac standing beside him. His heart felt heavy as he drove out of town. As if on autopilot he found himself at the falls, not to find answers but to maybe get a little peace. He felt like being there would make him feel closer to her somehow, so he let his heart lead and prayed God would take care of the rest.

Why Mac

The walking trails at the falls were not as populated as the downtown street for the sales event. The biting cold usually kept the tourist away from her small mountain town. The fall of the year was another story because Mac's sweet, quaint hometown was what existed in the mind of dreamers, straight from a postcard. While the tourists went down to Florida to catch the warmer weather, they missed one of the most beautiful mountain seasons, beautiful that is if one were equipped with chains on tires and a fierce determination to stick it out.

There was nothing like a cascading and icicle laden waterfall in winter. Jordan's feet crunched on the packed snow, and he looked behind at his boot marks. Usually they would have two sets of tracks, with small markings of Jolly's snow booties she made him wear to protect his paws.

The wedding was to take place along the bridge, and he wanted to walk the steps one more time before his family and friends were around. The quiet of the day welcomed him. He pushed some of the snow away from the wood and leaned against the railing of the bridge.

Mac wanted this very angle because she said the Lord's decorations were the perfect backdrop for all their pictures. She knew what she was talking about because it was a majestic scene. He breathed deeply and tried to take in the moment, but his mind wasn't steady and he felt his core shaking.

The wedding was economical for sure, and that fit his financial sensibilities perfectly. He knew how much his parents had spent on their wedding because it was close to his mother pulling out a notebook, with receipts to prove it, that it was over thirty thousand dollars from start to finish. Jordan saw how his parents' marriage turned out. Money was the root cause of most of their problems from what he could piece together from their broken relationship.

"Lord, please bring her back safe," he whispered.

"She's fine, Jordan."

The voice startled him. It wasn't the same as the closet, it was a male voice.

"I thought you'd left."

"Well, I guess I needed to come back." Chancellor leaned against the railing with Jordan. "The Lord hears you calling, Jordan. You've got a direct line to the Master. I was right in the middle of a new dig when…poof…I'm here."

"So, you go back to what you were doing as if you were blinking?"

"Funny how no one seems to notice I'm gone. I guess they figure I take a lot of bathroom breaks. I still get the job done at the end of the day so that's probably why no one questions me."

"I have so many questions."

"Still? I thought I covered all the bases."

"Why Mac?

"Why is that cardinal red over there and not blue? Why does the snow fall in winter and not June? I can't answer the questions of why God chooses the colors or the seasons or us for missions. He just does."

"I have an idea. It's her heart. It has to be. Mac has a heart for people. For me. She saved me."

"God saved you. Mac was an instrument leading you closer to His presence."

"What's happening to Mac? Do you know?"

"She's fine, I'm telling you now. I've already checked up on the mission, and she seems perfectly at ease. Like a pro. She was a sweet thing. She talked of you, Jordan. She said she was marrying you in a day. Her eyes were filled with love. That's all you need to know."

"Waiting isn't easy, Chancellor."

"It never is for those on the other end of the waiting. But there is a purpose, I do know that. It should help you to be a little bit more understanding and patient."

"I think I need to be praying for the patience part. How about my life with Mac? Have you seen that?"

"I see a man in love with a traveler."

"That you do."

"Have faith, Jordan."

"I've heard that before."

"Because that's all you need."

Chancellor was gone, and if Jordan didn't see the indention of the snow on the railing where he was propped beside him, he wouldn't have believed the conversation happened.

"If it's that easy, Lord, then why can't Mac appear right here, give me a kiss, and then move back to whatever it is you have for her?"

As soon as he said it, he thought he got a hint of her perfume in the air. Her Japanese blossom smell was right by him, and he stepped closer to it.

"Mac. Are you here? Mac?"

An elderly man out for his morning walk said, "Did you lose someone?"

"You could say that."

"I know the feeling. My wife traveled on, and one day I know I'll see her again. There's comfort in that."

Jordan said, "Yes, there is. I'm waiting."

"Are you a widow?"

"No. I'm getting married tomorrow."

"I remember my wedding day like it was yesterday. I took my little beauty right up to the judge's house and married her in the foyer of his estate. My mother went with us but had curlers in her hair. That should tell you something."

Jordan laughed at the thought of it. And he thought his mother was a little extreme. "That made for a picture, I'm sure."

"I was so excited to be marrying my gal, I left the license on his fancy dining room table. I didn't care about my mother's sponge rollers. I was a kid in a candy store. We were married 52 years, and she passed last year. We have five children and twelve grandchildren, all living in Crystal Falls because I guess they can't get enough of our stories. She loved these falls, and that's why I still come here even though my joints will pay for it later."

"Any advice for me? After 52 years, I'm sure you have a word or two."

"Don't waste a single day on anger. Tell that girl she's your world and mean it. Listen to her. You might not always be able to fix it but holding her hand matters when you can't."

"I'll remember that." Jordan watched him tip his hat and then turn to move on about his way. He had an idea.

"Hey, sir. What's your name?"

The man turned back to grasped Jordan's hand firmly. "Well, seems like before I told you my whole life story, I could've introduced myself. I'm Bill Watson."

"Mr. Bill, I would love it if you would attend my wedding tomorrow? Right here at the falls." He looked down at his watch. "We'll be gathering at one at this very spot. About this very time."

"An invitation? I haven't had one of those in quite some time."

"Well, it's nothing fancy. We are saying I do, and then hiking down to the Falls Center Complex for us to have our reception."

"Sounds very nice. I'd love to meet this lady of yours."

"She's worth waiting for, I tell you."

"I bet so, son. Well, I'll have to go get my best suit pressed this afternoon if I'm going to a snazzy to-do. Any single ladies there?"

"Maybe a few," Jordan said. "I'll make sure to introduce you if I come across one."

"Sounds like a plan. My gal would want me to be happy. She used to fuss I better get me another cutie after she's gone. She said I had enough love in me to make another woman happy. That's unselfish of her, don't you think?"

"She must have been special."

"Sure was. The specialist. It's been over a year. I can admit it gets lonely. But don't mind my mood. It's celebration time for you."

"Jordan. Jordan McLaughlin. It's nice to meet you."

"And you."

"See you and Mac on the bridge at one," he said as he made his way back down the bridge. Jordan could see his shoulders weren't as slumped as they were before.

Jordan hadn't remembered saying Mac's name aloud when he was talking with Mr. Bill. Maybe he recognized him from town. Everyone knew Mac and the Hart family.

"I hope you do," he muttered in return, but the wind carried it away.

∞∞∞

After Jolly had his walk and was down for the count, Jordan pulled out the box where he found Mac's letter. He was looking for signs, but there was nothing else left for him to discover. No words from her, no photographs. Only the paper front and back where they'd corresponded miraculously through time. It would've been so reassuring to find more evidence Mac was okay, but he knew none would probably appear right in front of his eyes. Maybe this was the way God was going to train him into some patience.

His mother texted him for confirmation for the address to the reception hall. She'd rented a party bus for their family to get to the rehearsal, and to stick around until it was over. Jordan didn't have a ticket for it and didn't want one. His father and Mark were going to be turning in at Mark's nine o'clock routine he'd had since elementary school. Jordan knew being in a new environment would be difficult for Mark, but at least the inn felt more like a home than a hotel.

There was still no word from Mac when he arrived at the Falls Center Complex. They wanted to have the rehearsal indoors that evening to practice the positioning and order of events. No one would want to stand out in thirty degree weather under the stars.

Well, except him and Mac but they were being considerate of their parents and knew the indoor rehearsal would work fine.

Preacher McNeill was standing outside under the Christmas lights wrapped around the wooden beams of the rustic barn. Everywhere in Crystal Falls was decorated for the season, including the complex. It was once an old stable converted into a conference center, fit for rentals for weddings, conferences, and retreats. The owners were personal friends of the Hart family, so they outdid themselves with extra attention to the small details to pitch in to help make their wedding reception as painless as possible.

Jordan had so many people to thank tonight during the rehearsal dinner and tomorrow after the wedding. The whole town came together to ensure Mac had a day she would always remember.

Now, Mac had to experience it to remember it. He checked his watch for the hundredth time and Preacher McNeill joked, "You worried the bride ditched you?"

"Pretty much," he said in return, with the preacher not realizing how close he'd come to the truth.

"Shelby is something else. She's in there telling everybody this elaborate story."

He breathed heavy and heaved open the heavy barn doors. This was going to be interesting. "Let me see what she's stirring up."

"Some hocus pocus about standing in for Mac because she's off at some bachelorette spa retreat, but all of her closest friends are in that room. Mac doesn't appear to be the kind to not show up. Says it's some kind of family tradition. Are you two okay? I knew marriage counseling should've been required as part of our deal."

"We're fine. Thanks for the heads up," Jordan said. He found Mrs. Hart before anyone could have time to grab and question him.

"It's all we could think of," she explained. "It appears you're rehearsing with Shelby tonight. She's the stand in for Mac."

"No word yet?"

"Nothing. I'm thinking she'll bust in at any minute and call this whole thing shenanigans what Shelby has concocted, and we go about our night as planned. I've already picked up the dress. It's ready for Mac tomorrow. No worries, dear. It's bound to be a surprise when she does appear, and it'll make for some grand entrance."

The music started to play over the speakers as the guests arrived. His mother did her small talk with Mrs. Hart before finding her way to pull Jordan aside for a scolding.

"What is going on here, Jordan? We haven't seen Mac since we came to town. There's something not right about this whole affair. Is she having an affair? Are you two on the rocks? If so, run. Run, tonight. If she can't make it to her own rehearsal on time, can you imagine what else she'll be late to in life."

"Mother, you know how busy weddings can get. I'm sure you've covered some pretty high-profile weddings. Even small-town events like ours takes a lot of work. Mac's fine. We're fine."

"Fine is the word that means not fine. When I hear fine, I hear fire."

"Well, when I saw fine, I mean fine."

"Jordan, are you sure you want to marry her now?"

"You are started to sound like Dad. He had quite a lot to say to me this morning."

His father was settling Mark in at the dining table reserved for family. Mark caught his eye and waved frantically at him. Jordan smiled and waved back. He was glad he'd get a place beside his brother tonight. It would help him keep his mind focused on the positive. Being around Mark always made him happy. Mac loved Mark, too. Once he could have sworn he saw Mark lean in as if he were about to hug her first. That would have been some day for Mark.

"Then, let me do whatever is opposite of your father then. How about you tell me if there's anything I need to know?"

"My life isn't some next big news story or some scoop for you to blast on the five o'clock news." He said the words again, "Mac's on a mission but will be back soon."

"Okay." His mother smoothed his hair down then turned away smiling and made her way back to the family. Whatever power was in those words needed to stick around as long as possible.

He whispered, "Lord, help me get through this night." Then, he had an idea. He took the microphone that was set up for the DJ and cut it on. "Does this work? Oh, okay. Now that I have everyone's attention. Mac and I want to thank everyone for coming to celebrate with us tonight. For everyone that's pitched in to turn this place into what you see now, a Christmas wonderland, we are so grateful. Mac is going to be so excited. It's perfect for her. Dinner has been provided by Sam's Catering, and we'd like to ask the preacher to bless the food. And for all of you who might be wondering, Mac's on a mission, but she'll be back soon."

Those were his last words about Mac, and the only ones he needed. The rehearsal dinner was filled with laughter, music, stories, and jokes. There were no more questions about why his bride was absent. It was as if the words themselves held the magic to give him the hope that even in her absence, her presence could still be felt.

Mac was on a mission, and she'd be back soon.

Call on Me

June was on cloud nine, dancing though the house like she was on stage at a ballet recital, with the grace of a star of Swan Lake gliding across the kitchen tile. Mags sat at the table with a box of tissues in her lap. Mac wasn't sure if it was for the cold or from her crying. The letter from her pen pal was propped on the kitchen table, and Mac knew she'd be delivering another letter tomorrow. Maybe if she were up early and did this final task, she'd be back for her wedding in time. She could play postmaster in 1955. That could be her ticket home.

Violet was finishing up the touches of dinner, and Mac didn't want to be rude but had to admit she had no appetite. It was her day to celebrate with family and friends at her rehearsal dinner. She was going to miss it. There was no flipping back or forward through time. She was stuck. She wished she had the knowledge of Chancellor Mackenzie and wondered if she'd ever be able to control her traveling.

As June talked all about her date with Stan and retold the whole night's events to them, Mac tried to smile but couldn't find it in her to do so. She pulled her seat closer to Mags and grabbed a tissue. Any minute it was going to rain, and she could no longer hold it in.

Mags put her arm around her to comfort her, and June stopped, breathless from twirling. "What's wrong? Mac?"

"I'm missing our celebration together. If my future time is moving the same speed as it is in this time, then Jordan was stood up at his own rehearsal dinner. He's going to be devastated."

"What if you try to write him again? He knows you're back here. Be strong, Mac. He's your guy. He's not going to be upset."

Mac wasn't as hopeful as June. She knew the life Jordan had led and didn't want to ever be the one to cause him any pain. He was a good man, and so wonderful to her. Regardless of not having strong relationship models, Jordan did everything with his heart. He loved her with a fierce kind of affection that made her warm thinking of it. He adored her, as he told her on many occasions, and didn't mind showing it. And he was at their reception without her.

Violet said, "What if we call on Chancellor again? Do you remember when we started to stir up his name, he came to the door like Mary Poppins calling in his fancy suit and hat. All he needed was an umbrella to kick off the show. He could maybe help you get back, Mac. I think your time here is done."

Mags said, "Maybe after you see Connie, you can travel back. Why don't you go tomorrow? Momma, what did Connie's mother say? Is she up for visitors yet? Has she been moved?"

Violet stopped stirring the spaghetti sauce simmering on the stove and wiped her hands on her apron. She pulled out a piece of paper and handed it to Mac.

"Here's the address to the hospital. We can drive you tomorrow after church. We'll stay in the car while you visit Connie. We'll be praying for her health and speedy recovery, and for you to get back to your time, too. That could be it. Mags might be right. A change might be coming for little Connie because of you."

June's voice was warm and encouraging. "You changed my life, Mac. Look at today. I've got Stan. I've got my man."

Mac laughed through her tears. "I heard that 'Stan Your Man' today and am glad I could help. As soon as I saw that on your papers, I wondered how that nickname got started. Now I know."

Mags squeezed her hand. "And you can help me by giving Connie my doll. Oh, I hate being sick. Are you sure the hospital won't let me visit?"

"No," Violet and Mac said in unison. Mac's voice was a little bit more forceful than it should have been.

She sighed heavily, and her hands wrung in her lap. "I guess after supper I need to work on my letter to her. June, can you help me find a good Bible verse I could add to the top. Like that's the first thing she reads when she opens it?"

June said, "That's a great idea, Mags. I'll help you. Mac, don't give up. This is all for a purpose, remember."

"I wish I knew what it was for."

Violet patted her shoulder. "Dear, I promise you when this is all over, I bet it'll be a wonderful surprise. It has to be something special if you're involved in it."

"I'm smack in the middle of it, and it doesn't feel so special. My heart is breaking for Jordan."

"Then, let's pray for Jordan. All of us. How about we sit here a few minutes in prayer. Let's ask the Lord to comfort Jordan and help him to see Mac has a mission possible, that only she can accomplish, and with the help of the Holy Spirit, it will all come to pass in due time."

Mac agreed prayer might be the answer. She looked at the faces of the family she loved so much. "I would love to pray with all of you."

She wanted to say so much to them, but words wouldn't come. She bowed her head and let Violet led them with a strong and steady voice, a motherly protective spirit covering them all as they sat huddled at the kitchen table, pleading for Jordan to have some peace while Mac was away. She felt Mags and June holding her hands, and then she started to feel a pulling away.

A distance. A separation. And she knew it was about to happen as waves upon waves crashed upon her heart. All her world went black.

God's Mission

All Jordan wanted was to see the end of the day. Mrs. Hart invited Jordan to come back with her and Mr. Hart and stay up to watch a fight with Mr. Hart. Jake tried to get him to go out with him for some drinks, even though he knew he wasn't the drinking type. Even in the midst of the chaos, he knew doing that wasn't going to solve anything. He could sense the vibes between his family and knew the air was so tense. In a time where he needed to draw strength from them, it seemed like he would be better to go at the evening alone.

He went back to the inn with Mark to settle him in for the night. Mark wanted to show him everything in the room as if he'd lived there forever and was the official tour guide of the place. His father asked him to stick in the room for a little bit with Mark, and he'd be back soon. There was a wine bar and restaurant connected to the inn, so Jordan figured he wanted to catch a break a few minutes while he could. Jordan didn't mind.

As Mark climbed into bed, Jordan flipped on the television and found a documentary series about animals. Mark loved to sleep with the television on. Jordan wondered if it helped give him the peace of security he wasn't alone. The lull of documentaries always put Mark to sleep. Maybe it was the soft instrumental music or the voice tones. He pulled the corner chair closer to Mark's bed and propped his feet up on the side of the mattress.

"I think I might stick around awhile, buddy. Is that okay?"

Mark clapped. "Jordan, stay."

"I think I might. I've got to go check on Jolly soon, and I'll see you tomorrow."

"Picture of Jolly. Picture of Jolly."

Jordan pulled out his phone and started to flip through his images. Many of them were of him and Mac. He wasn't too big on taking pictures, but he did it for her. She would say his camera was better, so he would be the one to snap and send them to her. Now he was glad she always suggested them.

Mark said, "Show Mark."

He pulled up a picture of Jolly and Mac and passed it to Mark. "There's Jolly. You'll see Jolly tomorrow. Jolly's in the wedding. You can help with him."

"I'll help with Jolly. Where's Mac? Mac Attack? Where's Mac?"

"Mac's on a mission, but she'll be back soon."

"God's mission?"

Mark almost dropped his phone. "What did you say?"

"God's mission? Mac's on God's mission?"

"How did you know that, Mark?"

"To set things right. Mac will set things right."

Jordan pressed him. "How did you know about Mac's mission?"

He shook his head. "No. God's mission."

Mark laid back on his pillow and then turned. He said, "God's mission. Mac's on God's mission." And he repeated it until he started to snore.

When his father came back in, he could tell he might have had a little more than he should have. Mark was out for the night, and he decided it was time to leave. He couldn't get it out of his mind how Mark would've known about Mac. Another mystery.

Jordan drove to Mac's and found Jolly waiting for him by the door. "I know, Santa Man. I left you a little longer than normal. I'm sorry. Come on and let's go out back."

Jordan led Jolly to the back and he stood by the door. He watched the snow lightly falling, and he caught some in his hand. Everything beautiful always disappeared right before his eyes. Jolly bounded up, and he must have sensed his mood because he leaned in on his leg.

"You miss her, too. I know. Life isn't right without her."

"Without who? You better not have found someone while I was gone."

He turned and saw Mac standing in the kitchen. She was wearing a fifties style dress. Her cheeks were flushed red, her curly hair was wind whipped. He couldn't have stopped the tears if he tried. So, he didn't bother to.

Jordan found his way to her in two steps and crushed her against him. "I love you, woman."

"And I love you. Oh, Jordan. You won't believe what's happened."

"Let me hold you. We've got time for all of that later."

"That's the problem," she said as she pulled herself away to look into his eyes. Her hands found his cheeks and her tone grew serious. "I don't know if we do."

"What does that mean?"

"I'm stuck there, Jordan, and I don't see a way out. I thought I was coming back to you but as soon as my feet hit the floor, I feel the tearing away again. Taking me back."

Jolly was almost knocking them over for attention from Mac. They made their way to the den, and Jordan couldn't keep his hands from touching her. He moved from her face, to her arm, to finally taking both hands in his. He remembered the words of Mr. Bill. If he couldn't solve it, at least he could hold her hands through it.

"Whatever it is, faith is what we need. I'm trying to be strong, Mac, and that's all that's holding me together."

Mac's eyes filled with surprise. "Faith? You said it like you meant it."

"I do, and for the first time in my life, I know the thing you're facing can be overcome."

"I don't know my purpose there, Jordan. I'm supposed to know it, right? At first, I thought it was Stan and June. I thought that from the beginning, but it seems to be working out okay. At least it appears to be. I'm still here anyway, so I'm thinking that's proof the family tree is still intact."

"So, maybe it's over. Maybe you're here because you're finished the mission."

"But I can feel the drifting of my spirit going back It's pulling me back in the direction to them once more. I don't understand. Why can't I stay here? Do I not have control of this?"

"I think you go when you're needed."

"Did anything happen here? Anything strange? Did you meet anyone new? Did anything happen I should be aware of? Anything? Please? I feel the darkness starting to close in again."

"We met Chancellor, and there was a family." He wanted to run for the stairs and grab the picture Aunt Shelby left in a frame, but he didn't want to leave her side, either. "Maybe if I show you the picture that appeared on your Mom's mantle, then maybe you'll recognize these people. Maybe that's what you've got to do."

"I don't know. Hurry. That might be it."

Jordan ran up the stairs, and Jolly barreled behind him. He grabbed the picture and by the time he made it down the steps, he felt it. The absence of her.

She was gone.

"Mac," he called as he rushed to the den. "Mac."

He sat down on the couch holding the picture. Whatever was happening back in 1955 wasn't as simple as Chancellor made it appear to be. He called out to the empty room. "Hey, Chancellor. Can you go give Mac a hand? She seems to be in need of some guidance. Don't leave her to figure this out. She's running out of time."

Jordan wanted to say, they're running out of time, because within a few hours they'd be expected to be on the bridge saying their vows.

He could tell by her desperation she understood what all this meant. Jordan also knew she loved him and was doing all she could to complete whatever it was God had her doing back in time. She hadn't given up on them. She loved him.

He prayed and hoped it somehow got to Mac's ears, or at least she would know it in her heart. "I'll wait for you, Mac. I'll wait."

Missing

A trio of shocked faces met Mac on her return. She had a chance to see Jordan. He was taking care of Jolly. They were well. They were waiting. Mac put her head on the table and hid her face. Relief flooded her as the rain poured. This time the tears were of a happiness of seeing them but the emptiness was rawer on the return. It's when a weatherman calls a wintry mix but you missed the warning and you're stuck out in it. Snow and sleet. Soft then cutting. Melting her to a puddle of slush.

June asked, "Where did you go?"

"Home."

"And..."

"I saw Jordan and Jolly. I flipped by his side. I flipped exactly where I was praying to be. To see him, and it worked."

Mags said, "And I prayed you'd come back to take my doll to Connie. It worked."

Mac didn't want to let her know it probably didn't work that way. Maybe God was giving her an allowance of time, like tickets for a round trip visit since it was her first travel. Maybe He knew how much Jordan was hurting. Jordan might've been praying for her the same exact time she was praying for him.

Violet asked, "How was he holding up, dear?"

"He was happy to see me, and he seemed like he was okay, I guess. He said something about meeting Chancellor and a new family."

Violet said, "Then, that means he got some answers from Chancellor that gave him some peace of mind. But what about this family? Someone new in our family showed up?"

"I guess so. He said their picture appeared on my mother's mantle board. Seems like somebody met while I was here."

June said, "Maybe it's our children. It could be my children from Stan? Oh, I hope we have a baseball team."

Mac laughed. "Maybe that's it. Maybe there are more children. Who knows? All I know is seeing Jordan was wonderful and painful all at the same time. I could feel the traveling switch happening. It's the strangest sensation, but I definitely recognized it. At first, I thought I was fainting. Now, I know the signs."

Bruce walked in and huffed. "What's with the huddle. Women don't play football. You look like you're about to call a play."

"We are about to have supper, that's what we're about."

"I was assuming that to be the case. That's why I made my way into the kitchen."

Mac's voice was light, "You know in my time, men help with the cooking and dishes and cleaning and..."

Bruce said, "Stop pulling my leg, child. That'll never happen."

"My momma always said never say never. You might just be surprised how fast the change will come on."

Bruce went and picked up his plate and served himself. "I can show I'm not a brute, after all. I can serve myself."

Violet raised her eyebrows. "That's a start, dear. How about helping me clean up the dishes after we eat?"

"Baby steps, woman. How about giving me credit for what I just did. Besides, that's what we've got the girls for, to do our chores for us."

"Daddy, I've got a wedding to plan."

"And I've got a letter to write."

"So busy in this house on a Saturday night. I've got a show to watch."

"After dishes you do," chimed Violet, winking at Mac.

"Yes, dear."

"That's settled then. Extra points for our family for being forward thinkers. All thanks to our traveling genes and Mackenzie Hart."

"Thank you, thank you very much," she said, bowing her head in acknowledgement of a life altering new day for Bruce and Violet.

Even though she was changing lives, her position in time wasn't changing. She sat right with them and went about her dinner, listening to the goings on of the day to day of 1955, soaking in every ounce she could so she could share with her momma and Shelby on her return. Oh, how they were going to love all of this. But not as much as how she'd cherish the memories. Flesh and blood. Family. Not names on a tree diagram on paper. Her people. Her life woven in time with them, becoming part of their history, their shared story.

She announced after dinner, "I'm going back soon, and I'm sure going to miss all of you."

Mags said, "Are you sure you give me permission to write about you in my new book."

Bruce asked, "You have another book idea already? What about Mags the Great? I really liked that title."

"I think I'm going to do the time travel romance, all about Mac and June. I'll change your names of course."

June said, "Of course. I'd like to be called Praline. Isn't it such a fitting name for a princess?"

"Oh, I love it," squealed Mags. "Let me go write this one down. If I don't start keeping notes, I'm going to forget all of my ideas. Princess Praline. I love the sound of how it just rolls off the tongue."

Bruce said, "She'll have a book of notes before she starts writing a book. That girl never stops with a story."

Mac replied, "Keep encouraging her. She might become a famous author one day. Who knows the future of Mags?"

"Wait? You don't?"

Mac stopped and looked at Violet. Oh, no. Hope while there was breath, she reminded herself. "Even if I did, I couldn't tell such a thing." She needed a distraction and fast. What would Mags love? Oh, she got it. "Now, let us go have a dress up party."

Mags said, "What are we going to dress up like this time?"

"I don't know. I think we should raid the closet and create new characters."

Mags squealed, "Oh, that sounds fun. I already know what I want to be. Florence Nightingale."

Mac said, "Oh, I can dress you up from top to bottom to protect yourself."

June said, "From what?"

Mac wanted to say when polio creeps like shadows over their home, but she couldn't do it. If she told them about Mags it would devastate them all. Mags was the light of the house. She didn't know Mags' future because she didn't have one, and if they knew beforehand, it would be a life of constant fear.

Lord, what am I missing here? Help me find the answer. Why am I still here?

She followed Mags as she bounded up the stairs and made it to June's bedroom. Mags pulled out the department store dress from the Ivey bag. "Put this on, Mac. This is your wedding rehearsal night. I'd love to see you in it. We can make like you're the bride."

June said, "We don't have to make believe that. If you're a nurse, and Mac is the bride, then what can I be?"

Mags dived into June's closet for an idea. "Let's put on a play. Let me see what character you can be."

"Now, she's getting all theatrical on us," June said exasperatedly. "This will never end."

Mags turned from the closet and said, "Humor me. I'm sick."

"Don't play it up that much, sis. You've got a cold."

"And it's hard to breath and my nose is sore, and my throat hurts, so there."

"There," said Mac. She pointed to what Mags was holding in her hand. It was a black dress, with a pair of pointed shoes. "You can be the wicked witch."

"How about the good witch? I can do spells that make you feel better."

"No, you kind of cackle when you laugh and your voice already sounds like a witchy-shrill, so go ahead and exaggerate it a tad, and you'll be full on witch."

June's face turned red. "Are you serious, Mags?"

"It'll be fun! Let's play dress up. You can try to sabotage Mac's wedding, and I can come in like Florence Nightingale and save the day."

"With what?"

Mags drew a picture on a sheet of paper and held it up. "A shot."

"Oh no, I'm stuck with a prickle, with a needle…help me!"
She fell to the floor as if she were melting.
Mac said, "Who's the dramatic one now?"

Mags crumbled beside her giggling with complete joy and giddiness at the game. "See, I knew you'd play along with me. Let's get dressed up."

Mags found a pair of white dress gloves from her Easter Sunday outfit and wore her white tights. She had on a white flower girl dress she wore in her cousin's wedding the year before. It was a little shorter, but still fit. June made her a paper nurses' hat, and Mac told her all about the importance of wearing the mouth covering to protect from germs. She'd folded one of Mag's doll outfits, a thin mesh dress worked perfectly as a surgical mask. They tied it to her with a spool of ribbon June used for her hairbows.

Mac helped June get all costumed up, using some green eye shadow to smear along her cheeks for effect. Mac didn't want to tell June her laugh did cackle just a little like a witch. It was hilarious to see them all in the mirror together. Violet came in to take a picture of their costume game, and then decided it was time to shoo them out of Mags' room so she could go to bed.

Mac wanted to spend as much time with June as she could. "It's the night before my wedding, June. Can we stay up listening to records and talking?"

"We'll have to keep it down because we'll get up early for church in the morning, but sure. That sounds like an awesome idea."

"It sure does."

Mac looked at the clock on the nightstand and wondered what Jordan was up to. She was sure he was with Jake or out with his buddies from work. Maybe they had a late night get together of their own. Whatever it was that he was doing, she hoped he was thinking of her.

They played through at least one side of every record June owned, singing quietly to the tunes. The ones Mac didn't know, she left all to June. They both loved music, and history, and teaching and wanting to help people. She had so much in common with June. She always wished to meet her growing up but never had the chance. She reached over to give June a quick hug when the door burst open.

To their surprise, it was a wild-eyed Violet, wrapped in her robe in the middle of the night. "Is Mags in here with you?"

"No, she's asleep, Momma."

She started to pace the room. "I had a nightmare. It was of Mags running down a highway alone. I could see her waving at me, with a smile on her face, then lights barring down at her. Truck lights. Where's Mags?"

Mac sprinted to check Mags bedroom. She ran downstairs where Bruce was waiting in the den. All of the lights were on downstairs, and he was on the phone. Mac guessed he'd already called the police.

Mac asked, "Where's the paper with the address on it? Where's Mary? Where's the doll?"

"It was right here," said Violet. "I saw the paper still on the counter when I went up for bed. I figured we'd leave it there for tomorrow when we took you to the hospital."

Mac sat down hard in the kitchen chair, rocking it a little across the floor. "She's not missing. She's gone to visit Connie."

"But Connie has…"

Violet couldn't finish the sentence. June asked, "What?"

"She's sick, June. She's really sick."

"Then, we need to tell the police to look for Mags on the route to the hospital. Let's go, Momma. Let's get there before Mags does."

All Mac could do was pray. Could she transport herself from here to there with a thought? Was that how this traveling could work?

They piled into the Pontiac, and Bruce took a wild spin out of the driveway. "We'll make it in time," he reassured them. "We'll get there. I know it."

Violet said, "Let's all pray we do. Pray for Connie. Pray for Mags. Lord, pray for us. We all need a little seeing after."

"Amen," said Mac. She held onto June's hand in the backseat, as they rushed to the hospital. She remembered what Jordan told her, and she knew it was time to build it up. "Faith is what we need. It can move mountains."

She didn't want to tell them it could also save Mags. She figured they knew it could be so. She focused on the word faith. Hope while there is still breath. Faith to move mountains. She repeated it over and over until they made it to the entrance of the county hospital in Silver Springs.

Violet rushed in before them. She called out to the night guard. "Have you seen a little girl? She's alone. We think she came to see her friend Connie Cross."

"Hold on, mam. Hold on. Let's check the registry. Everyone has to sign in at the desk. Where's the night receptionist? Hold on."

The desk was vacant. The receptionist left a quick note she was on break and would be back soon. He went around and picked up the ledger. He looked for Mags name, but no one checked in. Visiting hours were over even if she would've tried.

The receptionist came from a back room. "What's up, Charlie?"

Bruce stepped forward. "Have you seen my little girl? She might be carrying a doll. She's about this high," he held up his hand right above his waist. "Her name is Mags."

"I haven't seen anyone, mister. Who would she be here to see?"

June said, "Connie Cross. Can you please help us? Can you give us her room number?"

"It's late miss. We'd be breaking hospital policy."

Mac looked to the guard. "Couldn't you walk us? With your keen eye, you could maybe spot her before we could even find her. Please help us, sir. She's just a little girl."

"I've got a little girl of my own. I'd want someone to help her, too, if she were in a predicament as this. So, she left the house without you knowing? Smart young thing to make it to the hospital."

"We're in the next county over. It's her pen pal best friend for three years. She knows Connie isn't doing well, and she wanted to give her a doll."

"That sounds like a sweet girl."

Bruce huffed, worry clearly etched on his face. "She's one awesome girl, I'm telling you. And when I find her, she's grounded for her entire life."

"Alright. Let's go. I'll take you to the room. Let's see if we can find your daughter. What's the number?"

The receptionist said, "I don't want to get in trouble."

"I'll take the heat for this if it comes out," answered the guard. "Tell us the number."

She slid the book over and pointed to room 273.

"Thank you, kindly," he said. "Follow me. We can use the staff elevator."

They all got into the elevator, and Violet started to pray out loud. "Lord, help me find my baby. Let her be safe."

Mac began to pray as well. If only she could have had Mags with her and June. Why didn't they let her sneak in when she asked to stay up with them?

June was biting her lip with worry. "I hope Mags is okay. Traveling out alone in the middle of the night like this? I'd be so scared, and she's a baby."

The guard said, "Speaking from experience, sometimes the young ones don't see the danger like we do. That's why they need a little helping hand to steer them. She seems like she's trying to do a good deed. Just wish it would have been in the daylight and supervised."

Violet said, "You and me both. We made plans to come right after church to let Mac bring it in for her."

"She must have wanted to do it herself," answered Mac. "She's a little stubborn, it appears."

"Maybe a little like me," said Bruce. "I can take the blame for that."

"It's that stubbornness that can also make her strong," said the guard. "Come on. Let's see what's behind door 273."

They rushed to the door and then Mac remembered she was the only one vaccinated. She didn't want anyone to go in but her. She looked at Violet. "Maybe this is my mission. Can you please let me do this alone?"

The guard opened the door, and without another word, Mac slipped inside and closed the door behind her. She turned and saw three large respirators lined side by side. What she remembered of an iron lung in pictures didn't do it justice when she was standing face to face with them. The sound was the pushing and pulling of a vacuum suction, loud, rhythmic, and off set by the other machines. It was as if they were auditioning for a band.

Each machine held a child. A small boy with a dark, curly mop top had his eyes closed. Mac was sure he was asleep. The other girl looked as if she were a young teenager, and she was also asleep. Maybe the sound would drown out any other noise like ocean waves. Mac crept to the last respirator closest to the wall and knew she'd found Connie.

Her blond hair fell off the pillow and cascaded down the side of the neck brace. She appeared to be whispering. Mac made it to the corner and saw Mags' white dress shoes and stockings before she saw Mags. She giggled and told Connie how they'd played dress up earlier, and she wanted to play real life nurse with her to make her feel better.

Mac put her hand over her mouth to stifle a cry. *Lord, help this child. These children.* "Hey, Mags."

Mags came around and gave Mac a huge hug. "Meet my best friend, Connie. This is Mac, my great-great niece."

The girl struggled to breath and it sounded loud then soft as the machine did its work. "It's nice to meet you."

"You, too. We've been worried sick about Mags. She took off in the night."

"It sure was an adventure. I'm sorry I had y'all upset. Am I going to be punished?"

"Probably," said Mac. "Did you bring Mary?"

"Yes, but I can't give it to her. Her hands are in these holes and it's not big enough to fit the doll inside."

Connie smiled when Mags showed her the doll again. "I love it. She's beautiful."

Mac said, "We can leave it by the table. I'm sure you can tell your mother in the morning how a smart, young nurse came in and left it for you."

Mags smiled. "Do you like my uniform? I kept on the gloves and the face mask and everything like we played earlier. I thought it would surprise Connie. It worked, too. Can you believe she fell for the disguise and figured I was a short nurse? I fooled her."

"You sure did. When you said it was you, I thought I'd just fall out. Well, not literally. I'm pretty stuck in this thing, but you know what I mean. I'll cherish Mary forever and the memory of you sneaking in here in the middle of the night. Classic. As soon as I get out of here, I'll start writing you again. I hope you understand why I haven't."

"I'll write to you anyway. I've got so much to tell you. Can you believe the other day that Bill Watson..."

Mac turned from them and let the girls whisper in the night. She positioned the doll on the table by the window and grabbed a pen and paper to write a note that the doll was meant for Connie, so no one would take it away.

"I think it's time to go, Mags. Tell your friend you'll see her soon."

"Until we meet again," said Mags, and she waved at Connie.

Connie blinked her eyes in return and repeated, "Until we meet again."

Mags took Mac's hand and said before opening the door, "Now, I hope I'm not in too much hot water."

Mac smiled. "I'll tell them it was worth it."

But before she could say another word or plead Mag's case, she felt her body releasing from time and space. It was happening. She wanted to give them all hugs and tell them how much she loved them. But the darkness was closing in, and she felt as if she was falling through a tiny tunnel, being forced through.

She felt the last squeeze of a tiny hand grasped in hers, and the calling of her name. She had no power within her to call back or say goodbye. Her mission was complete. She was going home.

About Time 

Loving a traveler wouldn't be easy, but Mac was worth it all. Jordan texted Jake to meet him at the falls. Everyone would arrive soon, and he held out at Mac's as long as he could, waiting for her return. He left her a note on the stationary that worked magic before, just in case she could find it in her time, and if she appeared when he left, she'd know what day it was when she came back and where she was supposed to be.

December 21ˢᵗ – Our Forever Day
Dear Mac,
Meet me at our place. You know the time. I'm waiting.
Yours,
Jordan

The party bus was back in the parking lot. His mother must've seriously spent a lot of cash on the weekend. When they told her they weren't having any alcohol at the reception, he guessed she needed the bus in the parking lot for a quick run.

He laughed when he realized he scanned the parking lot for Mac's Jeep. As if she needed a car. *She's going to make it*, he thought. *It's going to work out.*

Mrs. Hart was dressed in an elegant emerald green gown with a long fur coat. His mother's high heels clicked to him, setting the tone before her voice hit his pounding head.

"The bride? Where is she, Jordan?"

"Mac's on a mission, but she'll be back soon."

She turned and smiled at his father. "Mac's going to be here soon. Do you want to take Mark inside?"

Mark stepped up and petted Jolly. "Help Jolly."

Jordan said, "Sure. There's not much to do, though. Just wait."

"God's mission."

"Yeah, I know buddy. Thanks for reminding me."

Mark stood out in the brisk air with Jordan and Jake. Jake kept reassuring him Mac would make it even thirty minutes after the time was for them to make it to the bridge. They gave up standing outside and made it to the reception hall where everyone was socializing and catching up. Some of his family hadn't been in the same room in years, so it was a happy occasion for them. None of them really paid any attention to the time or that Mac wasn't present. It was as if a fog were surrounding them all, except Jordan. Jordan knew her absence, and his heart was hurting.

There was no point in leaving the reception hall without her, but he felt the sudden urge to run. To remove himself from all of the joy he was seeing because he couldn't feel it. Mrs. Hart and Aunt Shelby came and put their arms around him.

Aunt Shelby said, "It's going to be fine, Jordan. It'll happen. Give it time."

"She's not coming back," he whispered.

"Don't say that," scolded Mrs. Hart.

Mark muttered, as he rocked back and forth, "God's mission."

Aunt Shelby's mouth dropped. "He knows?"

"Somehow, he knows. I didn't say a word."

Mrs. Hart smiled. "The mysteries of God's children. I am in awe of His handiwork every day."

Preacher McNeill came over, followed by Mr. Bill Watson. Jordan knew the questions were going to start all over again.

Preacher McNeill put his arm around Jordan. "Why don't we all start to take a walk to the bridge?"

"Do you know something I don't? Like when Mac is coming back?"

"I have a feeling when we make it, she'll be waiting. Just a hunch. Call it intuition, but I like to think of it as the Holy Spirit."

Jordan said, "Mr. Bill, it's nice to see you here. I'm glad you could come. This is my future mother-in-law, Mrs. Hart and her sister, Shelby."

Mr. Bill said, "Don't mind Preacher McNeill. He knows on good authority that Mac is waiting."

"God's mission," said Mark. "God's mission is complete. Mac Attack is back. Mac is back."

Jordan said, "Mac's back?"

"Mac's back," said Mr. Bill. "I met her on the bridge walking in. She's waiting for you, Jordan. Looking all pretty in a wedding dress. I'm sure it was your bride. Seems like we knew each other all along, son."

Mrs. Hart gasped. "We have her dress here in one of the back rooms."

"She's wearing your mother's dress," said Jordan. "She had it on last night?"

Aunt Shelby screamed. "You saw Mac and didn't tell anyone? Jordan, we've been worried sick. You could have at least told us."

"It was only for a moment, and she was gone again."

"Then, what are we waiting for," urged Pastor McNeill. "The sun will be going down soon and no one was expecting an evening wedding."

Jordan grabbed Jolly's leash and called for the crowd. "Thanks for your patience. The wedding is starting now."

"Finally," yelled his father. "About time."

"We agree on something. It's about time," replied Jordan, and he sprinted out of the room, with Jolly right on his heels.

At the spot where he proposed stood the woman of his dreams. Jolly barked at the sight of Mac, and she lifted up the dress to not trip as she ran towards him. Her converses weren't snow weather material, but she held her footing across the planks.

Jordan said, "And here I was thinking you were going to stand me up."

"Never," she panted heavy, catching her breath. "What a ride, baby. I'm sorry I'm late."

"I won't let you live this one down."

"I don't get a traveler's pass? A get out of trouble-free card?"

"Maybe we can negotiate all that later. Right now, I'm getting that paper that says your mine before you disappear on me again."

"I don't think I'm going anywhere anytime soon."

Jordan turned serious. "I hope not, sweetheart. I at least need our honeymoon. We need to build some memories together to last me for when you travel again."

"It felt like forever, but it was only a couple of days."

"Like years apart," said Jordan. "I was so worried."

"I was fine. I mean, so much happened, Jordan. It's so crazy. I can't wait to tell you everything. Even Bill Watson was here on the bridge when I traveled back, and he remembered me. Can you believe he remembered me after all these years?"

"He did. Seems like you are pretty hard to forget. I think so anyway. You are the love of my life, Mac. Never forget it. I still have so many questions, but they'll work themselves out in time."

"I do, too. Maybe it'll be my only call. I've learned that life is unpredictable, and time travel isn't an exact science where I can grab a book off a library shelf or search it online. No answers."

"I tried online. There were no answers I could understand anyway. I even called my professor. She had tons of theories, and I'm thinking we might need to pay her a visit soon. Chancellor made the most sense to me and gave me the way to frame it so I wouldn't go crazy waiting."

Mark was next to meet them. "God's mission complete. Mac Attack is back."

Jordan felt the joy from Mark as if he were as happy to see her as he was.

Mac laughed. "I love you, too, Mark."

"God's mission."

"Yes, I was on God's mission. I don't know how I helped, honestly, but I do think it was God's mission after all."

"Mac's back."

Jordan laughed. "I can see that, buddy. Now, while you're happy, come and give a hug to your little brother. That would be the best wedding present ever."

Mark rocked back and forth in excitement, forgetting all about him and only focusing on what was important. "Mac's back."

Jordan couldn't help but smile. "Well, maybe another time. Mac's back. Thank God."

Mac looked to the crowd. "Do you see him?"

"Who?"

"Bill Watson?"

"He's here, somewhere. He was the one that told me you were back. I just met him yesterday and invited him to the wedding. He acted like he didn't know you before. So, you met him on your travels, and I happened to meet him just yesterday? That's a little ironic, don't you think."

"No. Fate. It was meant to be. Did he have a young girl, I mean, an elderly woman with him?"

"No, he was alone. Did you figure out the family I was going to show you in the picture frame from your mother's mantle?"

"Yes, I can't wait to tell you about that. They should be here, too. I'm sure now that I'm back, they are a part of the crowd. It's all coming back to me in little pieces. I can start to see the color of it, and it's beautiful. Awe, Jordan. She's saved. She made it. Oh, thank you Jesus. She didn't die."

Mac began to cry and didn't care one bit that she'd probably looked a mess. She knew who could be waiting for her in the crowd of family and friends gathering around them.

"She's an author. There'll be autographed copies lined up on my bookshelf when we get back home. Oh, Mags. She made it. And the family, I see them now. Look, that's my cousin Jo's family, Mag's grandchildren..."

"Magic," whispered Jordan. "That's all I can say."

The preacher came next and said for the rest of the guests to hear, "Well, that rehearsal was pretty much for show. There's been nothing happening in order since the moment we arrived. We were the ones walking to you, Mac. That's a first."

Mac smiled. "And now that you're all here, I want you all to know how much I love you guys."

Murmurings of I love you traveled through the small crowd that gathered on the bridge and around the planks to the rock barriers. There were no questions. It was almost as if they were all under a spell, like they weren't aware that the wedding was even four hours late. Magic. Time travel could maybe bend perceptions of those around them. Maybe it was just meant to feel put all together again, when he felt like he could fall apart from it all any minute.

Preacher McNeill announced, "It's time to get the two of you married."

Jordan leaned over and kissed Mac on the cheek. "Since we are so out of order, I thought we should start it with a kiss."

"Well, if that's the case, kiss your bride, Jordan. A cheek kiss won't do."

"I've got to listen to the preacher," he said, and he leaned in to give Mac a slow, sweet kiss that took her breath away.

"This is truly a magical Christmas wedding. The one of my dreams."

"And you are the woman of mine. Let's do this."

Preacher McNeill began. "We are gathered together today, in the sight of God..."

Mark said, "God's mission is complete."

Pastor McNeill chuckled, "Yes, sir. It appears to be true. God's mission to bring Mackenzie Hart and Jordan McLaughlin together as man and wife is being accomplished this very day. It's time to say your vows and pledge your love before God, family, and friends."

Jordan pulled her closer. "I'm ready."

"You better be."

Mark's large arms came around them both, and he pulled them together in a bear hug. "God's mission is complete."

Jordan felt the tears well in his eyes. Mac's shimmered in return. He felt the arms of his brother around him for the first time in his life. God could heal all things. God could create new things. He could also bring them together and keep them as one.

As long as they both shall live.

Sneak Peek Chapter One of Bridges!

Crazy Little Thing Called Love

Mimicking the same little sweet whine as his, I turned into the beggar for the tenth time to tell Alex, "Stop begging!" He would not leave me alone until I would relent to his wishes. Such a typical summer day.

Alex's chocolate-churned mocha eyes were wide as discs as he pulled at the hem of my t-shirt. "Please, please, please. Defeat this level, and I'll never ask you again."

I rolled my eyes as if to act aggravated, but I didn't mind. "Give it to me."

The game controller fits my hand like an old friend, and I crossed my legs on the couch to brace myself for the bouncing up and down of my ten-year-old brother.

Alex screamed as he flew punches in the air, missing my head by mere millimeters. "I knew you wanted to play. Kill those zombies, Jazz."

My body rocked from side to side, reminding me of our choppy boat rides across the inlet, and I left-handed him behind the knees to tackle him down beside me. He fell in place, waiting for me to get him unstuck. Alex always wanted mature rated games, which was beyond my understanding because they were always so tough for him, him getting stuck at least by level three. There goes big sissy flying into save the day and blast open a recon mission or decapitate vampires. Today, it was flesh-eating island zombies. Such fun I was having.

I had to admit spending time with Alex was a given for the summer. As I took down the zombies hiding in the forbidden mansion, I smiled at the reflection of his face of the flat screen. He was in awe of my skill and wished that I would stream. He was right. I was almost good enough to battle it out with Tucker and host my own *Twitch*. If I talked, that might have been a good life plan.

Speaking of the dreadlocked devil, he bounded in without knocking and said, "Hey, Grommet. What's up? Hey, babe."

He pulled my long, tangled hair straight out of my elastic band like it was nothing.

"Ow! Tucker, that hurt."

He winked as he made his way to our fridge, pulled out two Fizzes and plopped down beside me on his perfect spot to my right, making my body float again. I almost lost my balance off the couch and lost a life.

He grabbed the controller for me as I opened our drinks. "When did you get this one, Squirt? I didn't know it was out yet."

Alex didn't even flinch at all the names that Tucker had for him. In fact, thinking it over I'd never heard Tucker ever use his real name. When he first met me, he would always call me Jazz-line, and I had to constantly tell him it was spelled that way but pronounced Jazz-lean. He finally gave up and started calling me Lean Mean Green Machine, or Jazzy McMaster, or some weird name that made absolutely no sense. But that was Tucker, and we loved him for all of his silliness.

I told him, "We drove to *GamesRCool* last night and traded for it."

Tucker eyed me crooked, his blue eyes sparkling like the ocean. "Did you get it yet?"

I knew exactly what he misinterpreted, and it pained me to reply, "No car, yet. Luke dropped us off when he went to pick up some new restaurant supplies."

He put the game on pause, reached his suntanned bicep around my shoulder and squeezed me to the point that I was sure I'd bruise. He never knew how strong he was.

"These things take time, Jazz. It's all about the perfect moment with the perfect ride, the perfect wave."

Tucker jerked away, pushed X, and started the game back without breaking his concentration. For Tucker's sake, I was glad Murrell's Inlet, our little beach town in South Carolina, didn't have the big waves because he'd kill himself out there being a loony daredevil if we inhabited a place with decent ones. We were lucky to boogie board on a windy day. The South Carolina ocean was so calm.

But that didn't discourage his surfing dreams, and as soon as we graduated, he has promised that he's off to the University of Hawaii. It hurt at the thought of him moving across the continent and leaving me. Tucker had been my best friend since I was five years old. One more year. I shook it off trying not to think of what was next. For him or for me.

He threw the controller at Alex. "Here, Booger breath. I'm done. Level four is ready for your little hands." He pulled me up from the couch in one swoosh. "I'm kidnapping your sister today."

I tried to stop him, but my bare feet were dragging across the floor, and I was digging in. "Can't. You know I'm watching Alex today.

Alex cut off the TV and soared off the couch landing square on Tucker's back. "I'm being kidnapped, too."

His face grimaced and he made sounds like a pirate as he flipped him over, his Adidas shorts sliding down to expose his RAW boxers. "But if Monkey goes, then we can't discuss what I really need to talk to you about. And it's pressing. Like now. I mean today."

Great. I thought. Another girl conversation. Getting through Tucker's relationships was so taxing. That's why I never had one, other than the not talking part. But that was another issue altogether. I couldn't handle hard. It was painful enough being me let alone attaching someone to me like a leech. And when Tucker got a girl, she turned into a life-sucking amoeba, changing who they were to be who they thought he would want, within days. Then, he'd pull her away, flick her to the side, and find another willing leech.

I tried to pull Alex off him, but he was squiggling like one. "Okay, but we've got to drop him off first."

Alex, red-faced from the blood being drained to his brain, stomped his foot. "No way, I want to hear, too. Is it Lisa or Rhonda this time?"

Tucker shoved him through the door with a kick of his sandaled foot. "It's neither. Can we please go? This is important."

I looked down at my appearance and wished that I knew how to make it more presentable, but I wasn't equipped with that kind of information in my brain. It was too brainwashed by video games and horror movies to make room for girly thoughts on how to do my hair and makeup. Momma was always so swamped at Chica's, her restaurant that she and my stepdaddy owned, that she never had time to do the momma-girl stuff, like teach me how to apply eyeliner or blush. So, I was a mess most of the time. Maybe that was the real reason why I never had a relationship.

I pointed at the bright orange sugary stain on my shorts. "I've got to change. I'll be right back."

Tucker frowned. "Nobody cares what you're wearing."

"Exactly my point."

He looked at me confused. "Huh?"

I hurried down the tiny hallway of our beach villa, more like a tiny hotel looking setup with every single villa looking identical to ours with different shutters and doorframes. Thank God, that Tucker was the yellow one next to mine.

He yelled for the whole neighborhood to hear as he was chasing Alex around in our tiny front lawn. "We're waiting, princess. Your carriage awaits."

It was more like a deathtrap broken down 4X4 Jeep that he had to sometimes beat with a hammer to get the engine running. I grabbed an old pair of blue jean shorts, tried to brush the tangles out of my curly mess of hair that fell down to my waist, but without a wash and the sand still sticking to it from our sun up swim at the ocean this morning, there was really no use, so I threw it back up in the ponytail again.

I was reminded again that my two guys were out there because they were about to get the cops called on them for disorderly conduct if I didn't come out and break it up. Sometimes I wondered why in the world Tucker put up with Alex and me. He was so different from us. He was my sun, and I was his moon. He loved the attention, the spotlight, the heat. He was the party. The reason everybody came to the party. I was the one who never went. I loved to hide in the dark. I loved the cool breeze as it floated to me at night. All the noise of the day attacked my senses, and it was so hard to explain that to Tucker. He would never understand.

When took off in Jeepers Kreepers, what we nicknamed his death machine, I held on for dear life as we skidded out into the lines of beach traffic. I screamed over Pork Rinds, his favorite alternative band blaring from his playlist, "Why do you put up with me?"

He turned the volume down a notch. "What are you talking about, woman?"

"Why do you hang out with me and Alex?"

He switched it off and turned a little too sharp onto Highway 17 as I grabbed onto the roll bar for dear life. We were farther down the coast from Myrtle Beach, but the tourist still packed into our little inlet, especially during the motorcycle rally.

Tucker said, his voice picking up the most serious tone as he could muster, "I love you guys. Plain and simple like that."

I said, "We love you, too, but it has to be more than that."

I knew that he loved us. He never left us without telling us. No matter how big and goofy he was, he had the biggest heart of any guy I knew. Well, he was the only guy I knew.

"What's more than love? I've loved you since the minute I saw you with your pigtails and overalls punching Joey Paine out cold when he tried to kiss you under the art table in kindergarten. That sealed you'd be my best friend forever."

I knocked his shoulder and my knuckles hurt a lot worse than his thick skin. He had his routines, and they were more than trying to catch a wave and a tan, it was to tone for his ladies. "I'm really serious."

He sighed and said, "Stop feeling sorry for yourself, Jazz. You're my best friend, and you have to put up with me for the rest of your life or the rest of this year anyway."

I knew that he was referring to his college acceptance. He couldn't wait until early acceptance letters arrived. There it went again, my heart was in my throat, and I tried my best to push past the tears. Senior year would be harder than I ever imagined, and it had nothing to do with AP Calculus.

Tucker said, "Will you just shut up about this nonsense. I have something really important to talk with you about, and I need your help."

Tucker had so many girlfriends, sometimes more than one at the same time, with much dismay from my end, and he never listened to any of my advice anyway. I didn't know why he bothered to get me involved in his little childish escapades. But here I was again, dragged into another one.

"I'm in love, Jazz."

Alex asked, "What? With who? Is she hot?"

I'd never seen Tucker blush, but I was sure it wasn't that it was hitting 100 degrees; he was truly red in the face. Crab red. Tucker rounded the curve with a squeal of his tires and hit the employee parking lot with a spray of pebbles and rocks skirting away in fear. We both got out of the car, waiting on Alex who had his hands crossed in defiance.

He pouted. "You guys can't leave me hanging like this. Come on, Tucker. I want details."

And I was sure he did but Tucker was acting way too weird to discuss it in front of Alex. He never had problems showing off pictures of his girlfriends or parading them around in Chica's as if they were some new board of his. But this one must be different. It piqued my curiosity.

Momma was in the back, as usual, sweating it up, running up and down the line, pushing out orders and tackling lobster tails in one swish of her long, tanned arm. Everyone in town treated my chef-owner momma like royalty. She had a four-star establishment down by the waterfront, a daunting task to some with all our competition, but not for my momma. She loved the challenge and always strived for the best service, food, and atmosphere. She had a handsome, younger prince who adored her and treated her like a queen. Momma had her life. Sometimes I wondered if she ever included Alex and me in her perfect equation. It never felt like that anyway.

She gave Alex a quick hug and a peck on his full curly dark head, shaking it all out of order. She smiled at me and gave me that knowing look. It was lunch hour. They opened 11-2, then closed, opened again 5-10. She needed the extra hand, and without being asked, I picked up the salads and headed out to the dining room with a bright smile plastered on my face.

Hidden away in the corner where the crowds of hungry customers could fade away behind us, Tucker looked so uneasy as he squirmed in our family booth always reserved for us.

I put on my server voice, "Do you want something?"

He squirmed again and whispered, "Hurry so we can talk."

I shrugged. "You knew what would happen if I came here. She needs me. Can it wait a little bit?"

He looked down at his watch as if he had somewhere to be.

"Yeah, I guess. But I need you."

He had never was so serious before. This girl must be something.

"Just tell me her name. Who is it? "

"Bree."

I ran through the juniors and half of the faces of the garden tools he'd dated in the past and that name wasn't in my directory. This girl was a mystery, and she had captured my best friend. It's not that I was jealous. I never looked at Tucker that way, even though momma tried to encourage it more than once. To everyone else, I was sure they thought he was the finest thing to grace the planet. But he picked his boogers and farted way too much in front of me to see anything fine about him other than his fine smelling feet I swore he never washed. But I was a little stumped to see him this enamored, and then I wondered what he needed me for?

Momma needed me more, and for the next thirty minutes I helped her young college staff, Ruby and Peggy Lynn, catch up on lunch specials before crashing down in front of Tucker. Alex was running up and down the dock with his hacky-sack Tucker made for him, keeping our stepdad, Luke, busy laughing.

I pushed back my hair that had fallen out of my rubber band holder as I slid in across from Tucker. He leaned over, grabbed a strand and pulled on it. He always said he loved to watch it spring back in place.

"Okay, shoot. I'm here. Now, who's Bree?"

He grinned sheepishly. "You'll kill me."

"Oh, no you didn't." I kicked him under the table and he winced. "You didn't get her pregnant, did you?" We'd already had this scare last spring.

Tucker shook his head violently. "No way. I've not even touched her like that. No, it's not like that."

I sighed with relief and fell back against the leather-cushioned booth. "Thank God. Tucker, don't go scaring me like that. What is it? What did you do?"

"She's a sophomore."

That's no big deal. Why would I kill him? "So, there are seniors that date sophomores. That's not the end of the world."

He continued, this time pushing the salt and pepper mills around in circles, spilling salt. I picked it up and threw it over mine and Tucker's left shoulders out of habit. He still wouldn't look at me.

"Well, I've got a genuine problem and you're the only one who can help me?"

I laughed. "If you want me to rub eucalyptus in your dreads again, sorry."

His face lit up again remembering it, too. "I wish it were that simple. I need you to go out with me."

Okay, that made me spill the saltshaker. I threw it over my left again. "What did you just say?"

He said, "Hear me out, okay. She's fifteen years old and her momma won't let her out of her sight without chaperones, so I really need for you to be like my wingman for our dates and I've got to be with her, and I have to have somebody. And I can't ask Billy, Jamie, or Frankie. They would scare her away from me the minute she spends time together with that rough crew. You are my moon. You are my moon and stars, please, please, please be my chaperone for the evening or summer, or the next year, please!"

I frowned, thinking about how that would go. "Are you serious?"

He grabbed my hand and squeezed. "Bree is different, trust me."

I trusted him with life, and I knew that if I needed him, he'd do the same for me. So, of course, I could never say no, and now I'd be a granny chaperone.

"Okay, but wait, on one condition. If you start your kissing mess then you do it away from me. I don't want to be reminded I haven't had my first kiss yet."

His eyebrows furrowed. "Wait, I thought Joey Paine kissed you."

I couldn't help but laugh. "That didn't count. I punched him, remember. It wasn't mutual."

He leaned in closer. "Well, if I kiss you, will you be over it already."

He was so stupid and dramatic all the time. He needed his own one-man show.

"What would Bree say about that?"

Tucker leaned back, his voice confident and filled with emotion. "She knows about us and for the first time, it's okay. Thank God. You don't know how much of a difference that is."

"Ah-ah, I knew I got to those other girls and that was the reason that my popularity stunk. Nobody can stand it they are so jealous."

"The price to pay I guess, to be my friend. But Bree can't wait to meet you. She's the sweetest thing, besides you. When I told her about us, she was so cool with it. That's when I knew I could love her. That's why I've loved no one else. I couldn't help but love her anyway. She's it, Jazzy. Sorry you haven't found your it yet. I told you, I'd hook you up."

"My it would be some evil clown terrorizing me, knowing my luck. No hookups for me, thank you very much. Single and loving it."

He frowned and turned to look out the window again. My social status was always a concern for him. My school experiences had been less than lack-luster. Filled with studying, tests, reading, and hiding. No friends by lockers, no friends at lunch, no friends. Filled with teachers and Tucker. That is when Tucker could get away from his football crowd long enough to make plans with me after practice. No girls to talk with, to share secrets with, no guys to kiss. High school wasn't as it was in the movies for me. High school was a day-by-day existence to get me to graduation. What was so awful was that I didn't know what came next?

Momma was as concerned as Tucker was, I was sure. When she got a second to spend with me, it was always the inquisition. Why can't you be more like Tucker? Where is your personality? Where is your voice? What happened to you? Repeatedly. Tucker motioned for Luke, and I watched him pull momma out of the kitchen. They were both headed this way. Great. An intervention.

Momma smiled and kissed Tucker on the cheek. "I heard about your date tonight, Jazzline. It sounds wonderful."

I sighed. Great, they already figured I could not say no. "Sure."

Luke started in with his fatherly like voice booming a little too over the top. He had no children of his own, so he fell into us half-grown, but he did a decent job, to be honest. "Your mother and I think this is a fresh start for you. You need to get out and have fun. We want you to experience life. Going on this double date will be a confidence booster."

My mouth gaped open. "Double date? Tucker?"

He squirmed in his seat. "I forgot to mention that. Bree's parents won't let her go out unless her older brother goes. She has two brothers. I haven't met them yet, so I don't know what you're getting yourself into. but I'm sure if they are anything like Bree, you'll love him."

Momma chimed in, trying her best to put it on thick in front of her crowd. "It will be fine, Jazzline. You don't even have to like him. You have to go. One step towards dating this one guy will lead to other guys, and other guys, and soon you'll have a record of accomplishment like Tucker."

I laughed at that. Not in a million years could I ever catch up with him. Tucker beamed. "Thanks so much, Mrs. Chicand, for believing in me. I have changed this time. Brianna is the one."

Momma's eyebrows rose. "I can't wait to meet her tonight. Jazzline, don't even think about coming to the back and helping. We have it all covered."

I threw up my hands and sighed. Great. My actual first date, double date or whatever, and I would be at Chica's. Couldn't Tucker be more creative than that? I needed to queue Netflix's romance categories and try to get Tucker the hookup. At least I would feel right at home. The big goof.

Momma handed me a wad of bills. I wasn't the girl that had a credit card with her name on it even though I could have if I asked. I wasn't the girl that even had a bank account. Material objects meant nothing to me. But momma was handing me money for something, and I was sure it wasn't for my dinner.

Luke smiled and pulled me out of the booth. "Now get prettied up like your momma. We can't wait to see you fixed up. We're sure you'll be stunning."

Tucker said, "I'll get Alex. I can't wait to put him through all of this pain and torture. It'll be hilarious. Come on."

The wad of money was crushed between my tiny hand and his large calloused one. I murmured a thank you to Momma and Luke, and we were off hunting our little man to kidnap him yet again for a prettied-up day of fun.

When we made it inside Jeepers Kreepers, Tucker wished he were with a serial murderer I was sure, after I let him have it. How dare he try to push me towards a double date, which was different words than chaperone? And how dare he force a makeover.

But there I was, going into Studio 7, being dropped off by an elated Tucker who was past cloud nine.

I called out to him, "She better love you, you moron."

He grinned that boyish grin that every girl dreamed he'd flash her. "I'm betting on it."

Alex rolled around in the receptionist's chair flipping through entertainment magazines as I was being tortured to death, plucked, and hair blown. I couldn't help but visualize all of the girls in the world that enjoyed this kind of abuse. Then, it hit me. I was alone. I had no one to impress.

The makeup stylist commented that I had a soft, natural face. When I finally caught sight of myself, I saw nothing like the Jazzline I knew. It was a definite improvement before walking in.

Alex was spiking his hair out with some stolen moose, and I gave him the evil eye for us to leave before they noticed him. Tucker was right outside with front curb service, and he even jumped out and opened the car door for me. I gave him the most peculiar look.

He laughed. "I know. I know. I'm practicing for tonight. That hair, though."

I blushed for some silly reason. "Stop it. Who's this girl anyway?"

After a few beating-with-a-hammer attempts to start Jeepers Kreepers, he fired up the ignition, and we sped off heading to the mall. I told him to make a U-turn because I slipped the rest of Momma's money in a charity bucket at the counter of the salon. There was no way I would get a new outfit, too. Having my hair probed and eyebrows plucked was enough for a girl for one day. This girl, anyway.

Alex was back immersed playing his handheld video game, and Tucker began to tell me the whole story of how he met Brianna MacKenzie on the beach two weeks earlier. They had been on the phone every waking second he could talk to her. She was his love. His one true soul mate. Had he been dipping into his Momma's romance novel stash stuffed by the toilet or watching Lifetime? Where was my surfer-wanna-be, Rastafarian, alternative-loving player?

"So, where does she go to school?" Her name was still not familiar.

"St. James Academy. And her parents are filthy rich or something like that. She lives down at Pawley's Island on an oceanfront mansion. Sounds like a dream to me to be the poor surfer in love with the rich girl who has the entire world but chose me."

"What's with the parents and why do I have to be your chaperone? Like this really happens anymore?"

"I'm her first boyfriend, and her parents are super-freaky strict. She has to introduce them to me tonight, and I'm about to lose my mind. I've met no girl's parents before. And you have to come, too. See, they've been to Chica's. That was an in for me. That was a way to get them to even let me take her out. Nice to know you have influence somewhere in the world."

I tried my best to gain my composure. "Meet the parents, too? Come on, Tucker."

He knew how awful I was at talking.

He patted me again like a school kid. "It'll be fine. I'll be right there. Jazz, you've got to work on yourself. You take yourself way extreme and put yourself in a cardboard box under the pier. It's almost like you're some hermit crab."

I couldn't help but laugh at him. "You mean a hermit?"

He was so ridiculous at times, but to be honest, this time he was right. I never talked unless I was forced to. I never pushed a conversation or carried one through. People somehow read I was closed for business, and they left me alone, often hiding behind Tucker's massive frame and boisterous personality enough for the both of us and two more. That was where I liked to be.

"Whatever. You know what I mean. Everybody at Sea Side has to know that you're cool to be with me, but you're a freeze pop around them. They can't even get to see who you are because you won't let them."

I sighed, staring out at the traffic before me wishing that it would hurry up, so we could avoid this conversation. "But you know who I am. Isn't that enough."

Tucker frowned. His face was plastered with that concerned look again, and I hated it. "No, it's not. We'll be seniors, Jazz-a-licious. Seniors! You've spent all these years with nobody but me and little shrimp here. What'll happen after high school?"

He would be a marine biologist far away on some blue island shore. Me? I knew it wouldn't be a culinary school for sure, but Momma didn't know that, and I wasn't about to go there.

"No clue."

"I'm leaving, Jazz. You've got to open yourself up to other people, or I'll be worrying about you when I'm not here."

"What? Do you think I need a babysitter? I'm not the ten-year-old here."

He smirked. "Well, sometimes you act like it. You'll love Bree. You really will. She is kinda like you. She's different."

"What are you trying to say? That I'm different?" My eyes twinkled at him because even though he was pushing my buttons, I could never be mad at him.

They chimed in, and I couldn't help but laugh. "No. You're weird."

Maybe it wasn't normal to be so closed up. There could be other life forms out there that could relate to me, and we could be friends and hang out.

Tucker dropped Alex off at Chica's, then me at the house to change. I needed to put together an outfit but my black work pants and one of Momma's blouses would have to do. There was no way I would get dressed up for this.

The doorbell rang. It couldn't be Tucker. He never rang doorbells. Then, it hit me. Tucker had left me here stranded for this stranger to pick me up. When I opened the door, I tried my best to smile but it all came out wrong.

The guy was not what I expected, but then again, I didn't quite know what to expect. I didn't even know his name. He held out his hand to me, and I wasn't sure what he wanted me to do. Would he shake my hand or kiss it? So, I did nothing but stand there in front of him and stare. I thanked God that I knew for certain that this guy wouldn't be the one. It would make it a whole lot easier to get through the night. Then, I would get Tucker Lane for this. He'd be owing me big time. Like for the rest of his life.

Thanks for Reading

I would love it if you could add a review online! Reviews really help an author and thank you in advance for supporting my work!

I would love to see your photos with the book! Please share social media reviews, and challenge others to pick up the series. Don't forget to tag me @jenlowrywrites so that I can join in on spreading the love around!

Don't forget to sign up for my monthly newsletter at www.jenlowrywrties.com to catch the latest author news, contests, and more!

Patreon Behind the Scenes Author Life, Pajama Hangouts, Author Gift Boxes, and More at

https://www.patreon.com/JenLowry

Author Bio

Jen Lowry lives outside of Raleigh, North Carolina and is a proud native of Robeson County. She is the author of a YA contemporary fiction novel, Sweet Potato Jones (2020 with Swoon Romance) and the best-selling Everyday Mom Challenge series. You'll find her enjoying every second of life spent with her family (preferably in pajamas). If you ask her what she's reading it's probably more than one book. Learn more about Jen at www.jenlowrywrites.com and follow her online @jenlowrywrites.

Author's Note

If you, a friend, or a loved one needs help, please don't keep it inside.

There are family, guidance counselors, teachers, community and nationwide organizations that can offer help.

National Alliance on Mental Illness (NAMI):
https://www.nami.org/
1-800-950-6264
TEXT NAMI to 741741

National Suicide Prevention Hotline:
https://suicidepreventionlifeline.org/
1-800-273-8255
TEXT HOME to 741741

Atrium Health Call Center
1-704-444-2400

Mental Health Resources http://www.mhresources.org

American Psychology Association
http://www.psychiatry.org/mental-health/

www.ingramcontent.com/pod-product-compliance
Lightning Source LLC
Chambersburg PA
CBHW020328110726
47898CB00003B/784